MW00772278

USA TODAY BESTSELLING AUTHOR

RACHAEL BLOOME

THE UNEXPECTED INN

a
Blessings Bay
N O V E L

Copyright © 2024 by Secret Garden Press

All rights reserved.

No part of this book may be reproduced in any form or by any electronic or mechanical means, including information storage and retrieval systems, without written permission from the author, except for the use of brief quotations in a book review. This book was written without the use of A.I. software.

For film and TV rights: hello@rachaelbloome.com

Cover Design: Ana Grigoriu-Voicu with Books-Design.

Editing: Krista Dapkey

Proofing: Beth Attwood

Series Reading Order

BLESSINGS ON STATE STREET

THE UNEXPECTED INN

THE UNBOUND BOOKSHOP

THE UNCOMPLICATED CAFÉ

THE UNINTENTIONAL TEAHOUSE

For my countless blessings.

To my partner through all life's joys and heartaches—I'm so grateful you're by my side.

To my dear friend, Gwenn, for displaying God's love, goodness, and grace, even when times are hard—you inspire me.

BLESSING /ˈbles.ɪŋ/ *noun*: a favor or gift bestowed by God that evokes joy

Letter From the Author

Dear Friend,

As I sit down to write you this letter, so many thoughts swirl in my mind.

I think about how my own journey with fostering a child began so unexpectedly, months after writing about Abby, Logan, and Max.

I also think about my dear friend, Gwenn—the woman who sparked the story behind Blessings on State Street and, honestly, this entire series. She's once again battling cancer, this time stage four. While my heart grieves with shared sorrow, it's also greatly encouraged by Gwenn's luminescent outlook on life. In her own words, here's what she has to say about the days ahead:

"James 1:17 says, 'Every good and perfect gift is from above, coming down from the Father of the heavenly lights, who does not change like shifting shadows.' What a great reminder that everything good in our lives comes from God, who is always faithful and full of grace. May we always trust in God's goodness and be grateful for the blessings in our lives... May we be grateful for all of them."

As I read Gwenn's words (which you can find at blessingsonstate.com/blog), they soothed the raw, broken places of my heart like a gentle balm—a reminder that no matter what we face, God is good and faithful, continually offering us His unfailing grace.

Although we can't always see them at first glance, there are blessings everywhere. And that's why I wanted to set my new series in the fictional town of Blessings Bay—a place where blessings, both big and small, are brought into the light where we can collect and count them, like the shimmering sea glass washed upon the shore.

In this series, I don't shy away from the dark corners of life. We all have wounds and scars, as do my characters. But there is great power and joy in looking for the good—in recognizing the Lord's blessings and being a blessing to each other.

It's my sincerest hope that this story—and the ones to follow—will not only entertain, but will encourage. I pray they will be a blessing.

As always, I'd love to hear from you. You can reach me at hello@rachaelbloome.com or come say hello in my private

Facebook group, Rachael Bloome's Secret Garden Book Club.

Until next time...
    Blessings & Blooms,

Rachael Bloome

Special Bo

As a special thank you to my readers, I've created an exclusive (and completely FREE) members-only area of my website called the Secret Garden Club. When you join, you'll receive access to a wealth of bonus content, including short stories, extra scenes, printable recipes, and more.

Adding to the fun, the content is regularly updated, so you never know what goodies you'll find.

By joining, you'll also receive exclusive emails with writing updates, sneak peeks, sales, freebies, and giveaways.

I'd love to stay in touch. You can join here: www.rachael bloome.com/pages/secret-garden-club.

Chapter One

ABBY

IN THE LONG list of Abigail Preston's life complications, kissing Logan Mathews landed near the top. Somewhere between starting a brand-new business and unexpectedly raising an eight-year-old boy. On any given day, one would slightly out-stress the others, but today, her convoluted love life unapologetically slid into first place.

Elbow deep in lemon-scented soap suds, Abby furiously scrubbed an innocent loaf pan, wishing she could wipe away her agitated thoughts as easily as breadcrumbs. Almost four months had passed since she'd kissed Logan in the middle of State Street on Christmas Day. She could still feel his lips pressed against hers as light, powdery snowflakes fell from the sky.

Something about the way he'd kissed her—tender, searching, and hopeful—had made her forget every closely guarded reservation she'd kept stacked around her heart like a barricade. She'd wanted more; to see if they had a future together. But life and its many complexities had other ideas, abandoning them in the awkward tension of what could've been. She couldn't help wondering if they'd made a mistake.

"Yay! Pumpkin bread!" Max Bailey scampered into the kitchen, his scrawny limbs caked in dirt. He'd grown a full inch since she'd welcomed him into her home last December, and he already needed new clothes. His previous foster parents hadn't given much thought to his wardrobe, forcing Max's lanky eight-year-old frame into clothing two sizes too small. But Abby planned to do things differently. Even if, as a first-time foster mom, she had no idea what she was doing.

"Can I have some?" Max peered hopefully at the steaming loaf on the butcher block island, his huge brown eyes reflecting his bottomless stomach. How could such a gangly kid eat so much?

"Yes, but wash your hands first." She scooted to the side, giving him room at the sink. At five-five, she knew it was only a matter of time before he surpassed her in height. The thought made her smile, then immediately sparked a pinprick of guilt.

Max's social worker, Carla Delgado, had made the situation abundantly clear: This wasn't Max's forever home. Abby had merely been a convenient placement when his foster parents—and her neighbors—the Hobarts, vanished in the middle of an identity theft investigation, leaving Max behind. Carla still hoped to track down a distant relative despite the fact that Max's father had been lost at sea for months and a family member had yet to come forward.

Abby's gaze lingered on Max's sweet, soil-streaked face as he scarfed down a generous slice, and her chest squeezed all the air from her lungs. In a blink, he'd stolen her heart, and no matter how many times Carla reminded her of the temporary arrangement, she couldn't imagine a world without Max.

Or Logan...

As if on cue, the man who occupied her thoughts—both waking and sleeping—strolled into the kitchen, drawing her gaze with an irresistible force she still found startling, even after rote responsibilities had usurped all hints of romance.

"Wow. Something smells incredible." His rich baritone rumbled through her like waves on the beach, and the vibrations thrummed all the way to her toes. "Did you save me a slice?" He grinned at Max. His muscular six-two frame—a pillar of strength and safety—towered above the small boy as he tousled his shaggy brown hair.

"Yeah, but you have to wash your hands first. Right, Abby?"

"Uh-huh," she mumbled absentmindedly, fixated on the soil smudges covering Logan's jeans and large calloused hands. His tan leather gardening belt hung askew around his hips, giving his austere, ex-military posture a sexy slant. How did the man make dirt look so scintillating?

As the official caretaker of the large Victorian-era estate they all called home, Logan wore a vast collection of proverbial hats from carpenter to plumber to groundskeeper. Even with the injury he sustained in the Air Force and the sporadic muscle spasms that still plagued him, he worked harder than any man she'd ever met. Maybe *too* hard, as if he had something to prove.

The meticulous backyard and garden that boasted a breathtaking view of the Pacific Ocean was his pièce de résistance, and Abby never knew she'd find a rugged man wielding a trowel and pruning shears so seductive.

Oblivious to her shameless ogling, Logan surveyed the chaotic kitchen. Dirty dishes, scattered eggshells, spilled flour, globs of gooey batter, and abandoned cookbooks littered the countertops. "So, how's it going in here?"

Abby blushed, turning back to her sink of soapy water. "I'm making progress," she fibbed. In truth, she was no closer to creating the perfect recipe than she'd been yesterday. Or the day before. But she couldn't admit that to Logan. It had been his suggestion to turn the beautiful historic home into a bed-and-breakfast, and she'd run with the idea, impulsively deciding to open a full-blown inn, complete with themed weekends, personalized itineraries, and a gourmet breakfast featuring a signature dish. And not just *any* signature dish, the kind of culinary delight guests would rave about long after their visit. The kind that would bring them back again and again.

She'd naively assumed it would take her only a week or two, tops. After all, as a cookbook ghostwriter, she made a living developing recipes for paying clients. This should be a literal cakewalk. And yet, faced with creating the first recipe that would bear her own name, she'd come up empty. And the worst part? She was quickly running out of inspiration—and time.

"We're making good progress, too." Logan placed a proud hand on Max's shoulder, and the little boy beamed between bites of pumpkin bread. "We have a few more shrubs to plant and an azalea to prune, but thanks to Max's help, the garden will be ready for our inaugural guest on Friday."

"Our in-og—what?" Max scrunched his nose, confused by the unfamiliar word.

"Inaugural," Logan repeated. "It means our first guest that will mark the opening of Blessings on State Street."

Abby's heart soared each time she heard the name of their new inn. When she arrived on the doorstep of 1109 West State Street last December, she'd never felt more lost and alone. Her entire world had unraveled when she'd learned her late husband had inherited a beach house in the small Northern California coastal town of Blessings Bay—a house he'd kept secret from her for reasons she still didn't understand. To maintain his duplicity, he'd hired his ex–Air Force buddy, Logan, to oversee the property on his behalf. Logan—the most unexpected blessing of all.

He joined her at the sink to wash his hands, briefly brushing his bare arm against hers as he reached for the faucet. Tingles of awareness coursed through her, setting every inch of her skin on fire. She resisted the urge to splash the sudsy, lukewarm water on her neck and collarbone to cool off.

Moments like this one, when every fiber of her being wanted to inch closer, to feel his strong, muscular arms wrap around her and pull her against him, she marveled at how she'd managed to get anything done. It took considerable effort to remain focused on her main objective: make Blessings on State Street a premier destination and introduce her guests to the magical town that had changed her life.

When she came to Blessings Bay, she'd wanted a place to hide, a refuge from her pain. Instead, she'd found a family to call her own. Albeit a quirky, unconventional family she was still trying to figure out, but a blessing all the same. And she wanted to impart the same positive, uplifting experience— the feeling of coming home—to every single person who walked through the front door, starting with their first guest.

She'd booked Serena Scott—a famous travel blogger who went by the catchy moniker the Savvy Sojourner—for a complimentary week-long stay in her most exclusive suite. Most proprietors seeking Serena's stamp of approval offered the influencer only one night. Or a long weekend, if they were feeling generous. But Abby knew she needed to pull out all the stops if she wanted Serena to choose her inn over the countless others vying for her attention. How could Serena turn down an entire *week* for free?

Plus, Abby had sweetened her offer by promising Serena she'd be the only guest in the inn and would receive her personal, undivided attention. Of course, securing one of the top travel influencers in the country for their first guest came with some risks, but a raving review from Serena—not to mention all the exposure on her multimillion-follower social media accounts—would set them up for success. And Abby was desperate to succeed.

Luckily, she had an ace up her sleeve. Her best friend, Nadia Chopra, not only had impeccable taste and style, she made a living as a professional product reviewer. Nadia had graciously agreed to check in as a practice guest for a few days and point out any areas needing improvement.

Although Abby appreciated the advice, she had another motive for inviting Nadia. Ever since "The Incident," her stalwart friend refused every offer of comfort and commiseration. But Abby didn't buy her brave face. A person simply didn't survive that degree of devastation unscathed.

But how did you support someone on the path to healing when they wouldn't even admit they needed help?

Chapter Two

NADIA

NADIA CHOPRA INHALED A DEEP, cleansing breath, relishing the salty ocean air as she zipped along the curvy coastal highway. The change in scenery from chaotic, congested Los Angeles was exactly what she needed.

On her left, craggy sea cliffs dropped dramatically to the pristine beaches below, the smooth sand decorated with sun-bleached driftwood. To her right, fragrant redwoods and lush, leafy ferns hugged the two-lane road, stretching up the mountainside until they met milky blue sky.

Her cell phone buzzed on the passenger seat, and she accepted the call via her car's Bluetooth. "Hi, Mom."

"What's that whooshing sound? Where are you? Are you driving?" Her mother rattled off the questions in lieu of a greeting, and Nadia bit back a laugh. Even at thirty years old, she'd never escape the well-intentioned mothering.

"I'm on my way to Abby's for a few days, but don't worry. You're on Bluetooth." She rolled up the windows, muffling the pleasant sound of waves crashing against the rocky shoreline. "What's up?"

"I spoke with Ishani this morning. You'll never guess what she told me."

Nadia adjusted her grip on the leather steering wheel. "What?" She played along, although they both knew the answer.

"She told me you're considering an arranged marriage. My own daughter. And I had to find out from my sister. Can you imagine my surprise?"

She was imagining it right now. Her mother would be perched on her favorite chair with the custom Aztec-blue upholstery, staring out the window of their Malibu beach house, wondering where she'd gone wrong with her eldest daughter.

"I'm sorry I didn't come to you and Dad first, but she has a gift for matchmaking. You know her track record."

"Her qualifications aren't my concern. Don't you—"

"Want a relationship like you and Dad?" Nadia interjected before her mother could finish her objection. They'd married in India, after meeting a total of three times, and Nadia had never known two people more perfect for each other. And yet, despite their marital success, they'd encouraged her to find love on her own. One of their more glaring parental mistakes. Why couldn't they be like other Indian parents who couldn't wait to handpick their offspring's partners?

"Our situation was different."

"How so?"

"We were..." Her mother trailed off, as if searching for the right word. After a thoughtful pause, she added softly, "Ready." Nadia winced. *Beta*, her mother said gently, evoking an endearment that meant *child*, "don't you think it's too soon for something like this? It's only been a few months since Brian—"

"Mom, I'm fine. Honestly." As a general rule, she didn't believe in lying. In fact, most people would argue she was honest to a fault. But sometimes, if you told a lie long enough, and with enough fervor, you could make it come true. As long as someone, like an overly concerned mother, didn't poke too hard at your flimsy facade.

Thankfully, a road sign welcoming her to Blessings Bay offered a much-needed escape, and she flicked on her blinker. "Mom, I'm sorry, but I need to get going. I'm almost at Abby's."

Her mother's heavy sigh filled the stereo speakers. "Okay, sweetheart. Give Abby my love."

"I will." Ending the call with a quick goodbye, she turned off the highway down a narrow lane that led to Main Street, a charming thoroughfare with colorful Victorian-style storefronts on one side and the vast Pacific Ocean on the other.

The first and last time she'd visited Abby in Blessings Bay had been right before Christmas. The quaint mom-and-pop shops had been bedecked in festive garb, and the long grassy promenade facing the picturesque seascape had boasted an enormous evergreen tree draped in twinkling lights.

Now, bathed in the burgeoning beauty of spring, the pretty pastel storefronts in lemon, sage, periwinkle, and rose-petal pink shone to perfection amid lilac, larkspur, and jasmine blossoms. No wonder Abby wanted to call this place home.

Turning right at the single stop sign, she eased onto State

Street, a wide road flanked by gorgeous historic homes in storybook styles like Queen Anne and Eastlake, with large wraparound porches, turrets, and gabled roofs.

The most beautiful home on the block belonged to Abby. The soft blue color reminded her of both the sea and sky—a fitting combination considering the two-story gem sat high on a bluff overlooking the ocean.

She'd been almost as shocked as Abby when the stuffy estate lawyer revealed her friend's late husband, Donnie, owned a secret beach house. She'd asked her then-boyfriend, Brian, if he knew about it, certain he'd been privy to Donnie's deceit. Two peas in an adrenaline-junkie pod, they'd bonded the day they met as test pilots at Edwards Air Force Base and had been inseparable ever since. In fact, they'd been together the day she met Brian, when he'd used his persuasive charm to finagle her phone number while she waited in line at her favorite coffee shop. Surely after all they'd been through, Donnie would've confided in Brian. But her ex swore up and down he had no idea. Of course, come to find out, he'd lied about a lot of things. What's one more deception added to the pile?

Nadia parked her sleek black Mercedes beside Abby's silver sedan in the driveway, and before she'd climbed out of the driver's seat, her friend bounded down the front steps, glowing like a welcome beacon. Flour dusted her apron and streaked her dark shoulder-length waves, and Nadia had a feeling she'd find smudges on her blouse once Abby relinquished her rib-crushing hug.

"I'm so glad you're here!" Abby took a step back to regard her at arm's length, concern reflecting in her large, expressive eyes.

"Before you ask"—Nadia held up a hand to stave off the pity—"I'm perfectly fine. I'm not here to wallow. I'm here to help my best friend open her soon-to-be award-winning inn."

"Can't we do both? I have plenty of delicious, wallow-worthy ice cream in the freezer, and I stocked up on Kleenex. I thought we could rewatch *The First Wives Club* and plot our hypothetical revenge on He Who Shall Not Be Named."

Nadia couldn't help a smile. "While that's tempting, I'm honestly doing okay. More than okay. Work's been great, and I finally feel like my life's back on track." She grabbed her favorite Chanel suitcase from the trunk, praying her declaration sounded convincing.

Abby cocked her head, her brow creased by a skeptical squint. Almost as if she knew Nadia still had nightmares about New Year's Eve.

"At the very least," Abby relented, "have some tea with me. I couldn't find all the spices your mom uses for her chai, but I did my best to match her recipe as closely as possible."

Nadia's heart warmed at the thoughtful gesture. "Tea sounds lovely. Thanks."

Leaving her suitcase in the foyer, she followed Abby into the kitchen, then halted abruptly. "What happened?"

A sheepish blush swept across Abby's cheeks. "I'm working on a signature dish for the inn."

"And your pantry exploded?"

"I suppose it looks that way, doesn't it?" Abby side-stepped a smattering of flour speckling the hardwood floor, maneuvering toward the pot of fragrant tea simmering on the stove.

"You realize this wouldn't pass a health inspection,

right?" Nadia wrinkled her nose at a pile of discarded banana peels.

"I know, I know." Abby poured the steaming liquid into two matching teacups, balancing the eclectic aroma of her many failed culinary attempts with the spicy sweetness of cinnamon, cloves, and cardamom. "I got a little carried away."

"More like obsessive," Nadia corrected. Abby had a tendency toward perfectionism and could get a little too caught up in the pursuit.

"Maybe," she conceded. "But with good reason. And don't worry. I have a few more recipes I want to try, then this place'll be spotless." She shoved aside a teetering stack of cookbooks cluttering the antique kitchen table before gesturing to Nadia to join her in the cozy breakfast nook.

"What about the recipe box Logan gave you for Christmas? You made his collection of old family recipes sound like the Holy Grail. I'm surprised you didn't find anything in there. Or a decent starting point, at least."

Abby glanced over her shoulder at a small wooden box on the counter, tucked between an electric kettle and ceramic cookie jar before dragging her attention back to the aromatic tendrils of steam curling from her teacup. "I... uh, haven't tried any of the recipes yet."

"What? Why not?"

"I don't know." Abby squirmed.

"Yes, you do. Spill it."

Abby sighed and finally met her gaze. In a feather-soft voice, tiptoeing toward a whisper, she murmured, "What if I find exactly what I'm looking for?"

"Then we celebrate."

When her friend didn't respond, and looked even more dejected, Nadia pressed further. "I don't understand, Abs. Isn't that what you want?"

"I thought it was. But now, I'm not so sure." Her shoulders slumped as if the weight of her heavy heart had crushed her slight frame.

"Is this about Donnie?" Nadia asked gently. "Because you know he'd want you to be happy." They'd shared many late-night phone calls as Abby wrestled with her love and loyalty for her late husband and her ever-increasing feelings for Logan. But Nadia thought she'd worked through a lot of those emotions.

"I know. It isn't Donnie. It's..." She bit her bottom lip, struggling with her next words. "It's Logan. What if I find the perfect recipe, but he regrets giving them to me? I can't use his grandmother's legacy. Not if he's changed his mind."

The loaded question lingered in the air between them, its gravity belied by the cheerfully chirping birds just beyond the bay window.

She had no idea Abby had doubts about her relationship with Logan. Sure, they'd had a rocky start. Most fairy tales didn't begin with the damsel in distress mistaking the hero for a burglar only to tase him senseless. But in the last few months, they'd grown close. They'd not only become business partners in the inn, they were the most amazing co-parents to Max. Logan had stepped in as a father figure the second Abby took on the role of foster mom, providing Max with a secure, loving home. Together, they made an incredible team. What had changed?

"What happened, Abs?"

"It's more like what *hasn't* happened." Abby tapped her fingertips against the porcelain teacup, her nerves on full display. "I think he might have second thoughts. About me. About us."

Nadia didn't believe it for a second. She'd seen the way Logan looked at her friend. His guarded stoicism melted into a puddle in Abby's presence. "What makes you think that?"

"Because we've been at a standstill since December. We never even talked about the kiss." Her incessant tapping sloshed hot tea over the rim, and she winced, licking her finger. "I don't know, Nadia. I think maybe it's all too much for him. The inn, raising Max, living together—"

"But you don't live together."

"Okay. So, not technically. But his bungalow is in the backyard. It's the same address. Plus, we eat all our meals together and most of our free time is spent with Max. What if he's no longer interested in me romantically, but our lives are so entangled, he doesn't know how to tell me?"

"Why don't you ask him?"

"And when am I supposed to do that?" she asked wryly, with a hint of desperation. "Hey, Logan, while you're pruning that azalea, is there anything else you'd like to cut out of your life? A slightly neurotic brunette, perhaps?" She flopped facedown on the table, elbowing the precarious stack of cookbooks.

They clattered in a noisy heap, and Nadia swiped her tea out of the way just in time. This was serious. Abby and Logan were the perfect couple. She could only dream that her aunt would find her a match as ideal as those two. And she wasn't about to let them mess things up over a failure to communicate.

By the time she left the inn, she'd have them well on their way to happily ever after. And with any luck—and some expert matchmaking—she'd be right behind them.

NADIA

THE FOLLOWING MORNING, Nadia jolted awake and ripped off her eye mask. Her sticky sweat dampened the supple, lavender-scented sheets, and she fought to kick herself free.

The nightmare lingered in her mind, blurring the lines between dream state and reality. Jeering faces stared back at her, faces that had witnessed every tortured nuance of her humiliation. And those words... those cruel, condemning words that echoed in a surreal amalgamation of Brian's voice blended with her own.

Nadia Chopra, beautiful but underwhelming. She did not live up to expectations. Bland. Boring. Basic. I do not recommend. One star.

One star, one star, one star...

The caustic chant still thundered in her eardrums, keeping pace with her hammering pulse.

"It isn't real," she said aloud, struggling to steady her tremulous voice.

Fleeing her bed, she padded toward the French doors and

flung them open. Escaping onto the balcony, she closed her eyes, bracing against the crisp, briny air as it chilled her flushed cheeks and assuaged her erratic heartbeat.

When she finally opened her eyes, she could breathe again. She fixed her gaze on the blanket of cobalt waters stretched toward the horizon. Soft morning sunlight glittered across the surface, guiding the waves toward shore.

She'd grown up by the ocean, but never appreciated the privilege. In LA, the beach was a status symbol—something to own. People boasted about their home's proximity at parties while rarely stepping foot on the sand. Its splendor had been commercialized and commoditized. But here, along the rugged Northern California coastline, the waters were wild, untamed, and unblemished. And something about its bold, unapologetic, blissfully unrefined beauty spoke to her soul, almost mollifying her fear of the murky waters. *Almost.*

Her spirit sufficiently quieted, she stepped back inside and dressed for the day, appreciating Abby's little touches of luxury. A thick, scrumptiously soft robe hung in the antique armoire beside the clothing she'd unpacked and slipped onto the fragrant cedar hangers the night before. She selected a simple spring dress that hugged her ample curves before falling midthigh and paired it with a cream cashmere cardigan and gold-accented sandals.

As she arranged her extensive makeup kit on the white porcelain sink in the surprisingly spacious en suite, she admired the clawfoot tub and basket of locally made soaps, lotions, and soaking salts. Abby had thought of every detail, and Nadia couldn't find a single thing she'd change. She had no doubt the Savvy Sojourner would be duly impressed.

As she descended the staircase nearly forty minutes later

—effortless beauty took time—Abby met her at the bottom with a wide smile and steaming travel mug.

"I thought we'd take our coffee to go and grab something to eat at the farmers market. If we don't get there early, all the best produce is gone."

"Works for me. That coffee smells sensational." She eagerly accepted the insulated mug, her mouth watering as delicious notes of chocolate and nutmeg wafted from the narrow opening in the lid.

"I guarantee you've never tasted anything better."

Nadia raised an eyebrow. "That's a bold claim considering I've reviewed exclusive blends that cost more than a bottle of Dom Pérignon, including the infamous kopi luwak coffee that passes through an animal's intestines."

Abby wrinkled her nose. "As delicious as that sounds, I'm confident this will be your new favorite." Abby watched as she brought the rim to her lips.

A burst of flavors both earthy and bright cascaded across her taste buds, drawing her into a state of caffeinated bliss.

Her delighted delirium must have displayed on her face, because Abby laughed. "I told you."

"You have to tell me where I can buy some."

"I'll give you the website. The roastery's in this small mountain town with the cutest name. Poppy Creek. Apparently, the roaster donates coffee to a lot of veteran-related charities. Once Logan heard about it, he wanted to give it a try. Now, he won't stop raving about it. He even got CeCe to serve it at her café."

"Where is Logan? Is he coming to the farmers market with us?" She took another sip, wondering if she could help orchestrate a few minutes for the two lovebirds to be alone.

Abby dropped her gaze, intently focused on stuffing her bare feet into a pair of worn slip-on sneakers. "He's gone. He left about an hour ago."

Something about the subtle strain in her voice gave Nadia pause. "Oh? Where to?" Blessings Bay was tiny, and ever since his injury, Logan didn't drive. There were only so many places the man could be, unless he took the bus.

"No idea." She shrugged and hooked an enormous canvas shopping bag over her shoulder. Next to her petite frame, the contrast in size would've been comical, except her pinched expression drained all the humor from the situation. "He disappears for a few hours every week. I asked him about it once, and he avoided the question. I haven't had the guts to bring it up again."

Nadia looped her arm around Abby's waist, summoning a smile. "Well, I'm here now. And you know there isn't a single topic I'm afraid to talk about." *Except for what happened on New Year's Eve*, she quietly added to herself.

Abby leaned her head against her shoulder. "I've missed you. Can you please stay forever?"

"I enjoy shopping way too much to survive in a small fashion-starved town like this," Nadia said with a laugh. "But before I leave, I'm making it my mission to get you and Logan to talk to each other. What you two have is special, Abs. Don't let anything take it away from you, okay?"

"You're right. Per usual." Abby straightened with a smile, her entire countenance brighter. "Ready to go?"

"After a refill." Nadia tapped her to-go mug, and following a quick top-up, they slipped out the front door.

At the same time, Verna Hoffstetter emerged from the house across the street. Clad in a purple pantsuit and matching cloche atop her short pumpkin-colored hair, the sprightly older woman perfectly complemented the lovely lilac-hued Queen Anne Victorian. A pudgy English bulldog waddled by her side.

"Good morning, Verna!" Abby waved.

"Good morning, lovelies." She met them in the middle of the wide tree-lined street. "Mr. Bingley, you remember Nadia, don't you?"

The squishy-faced pup sniffed her sandals, and Nadia bent to scratch his head. "Hello, Bing," she said, affectionately evoking his nickname. "How's life treating you?"

He licked her hand, wiggling his substantial backside.

"He loves the farmers market," Verna said on his behalf. "He's a big fan of the free samples."

"Any in particular I should try?" Nadia asked as they resumed their stroll toward the Main Street promenade.

"Oh, my heavens, yes! Tammy's Taffy is a must if you have a sweet tooth. And what woman doesn't?" Verna asked with a chuckle. "Well, except for Shirley Milton. The only sweetener she'll use is raw honey. And it has to be from happy bees, whatever that means. How can you tell if a bee is happy? The tonal frequency of the buzzing, I suppose. Maybe it's higher pitched? I'd ask Shirley, but then I'd get a lecture on proper hive maintenance and harvesting practices. And it's not as if I plan to become a beekeeper at eighty-nine years young. Wait. What was I saying?" She paused, then snapped her fingers. "Oh, yes. Tammy's Taffy. Tammy's son, Evan, usually operates the booth, and he's a bit of eye candy himself, if you like the blond-haired, blue-eyed, Robert Redford type. Not that you're in the market anymore." Verna gave Abby a gentle nudge, and her friend blushed.

"Are you still seeing that airman?" Verna asked, turning to Nadia.

Startled by her innocent question, Nadia stumbled on a nonexistent crack in the pavement. Luckily, before she had time to answer, they'd reached Main Street, and the hustle and bustle of the lively farmers market drew their focus to the festivities.

She'd forgotten all about Verna's eye candy comment until they reached the final booth at the end of the promenade. Colorfully wrapped taffies filled tall glass jars and spilled from white wicker baskets. But the man standing behind the booth stole the show.

Tall and chiseled, with the most striking blue-green eyes, he commanded her notice even in nondescript board shorts and a plain white tee.

"Hey, Verna. How's my favorite customer?" Eye Candy dropped to his knee to scratch Bing around the ears before pulling a dog biscuit out of his back pocket as if he'd been expecting them.

The chubby pup eagerly gobbled it up.

"Spoiled, as ever, thanks to you." Verna glowed with parental pride.

"Happy to do my part." The man rose back to his full six-foot-something of solid muscle. He wasn't bulky, but she couldn't help noting the crisp definition of his biceps. And she had a suspicion he stored a six-pack behind his thin cotton T-shirt.

Not that she cared.

"Nadia, dear. You have to sample one of Evan's taffies." Verna pressed a candy into the palm of her hand.

"I'd love to." The wax paper crinkled as she unwound the

twisted ends and popped the morsel into her mouth. A subtle sweetness of vanilla bean swirled across her tongue, the texture both soft and pleasantly chewy. "It's delicious."

"Are you sure?"

Startled by the man's curt question, she jerked her gaze to meet his.

He stared back with an icy intensity that caught her off guard.

"I beg your pardon?" How had she possibly offended him? Did he hate compliments?

"Are you sure it isn't *lacking in nuance and originality*?"

Something about his word choice tugged at her memory, and a sudden rush of heat swept across her cheeks. *Tammy's Taffy*. Now she recognized the name. They'd sent her a box of taffy to review about a year ago.

Oh, no....

She cringed as the pieces clicked into place. While she'd praised their use of real, natural ingredients and the texture of the taffy had been perfection, the assortment of flavors left a lot to be desired. Vanilla, mint, banana, and caramel. Nothing outstanding or noteworthy. The taffies had potential but fell short of exemplary.

She opened her mouth, but no words came out. What could she say? She'd given her honest opinion, and in her line of work—where reviews could easily be bought—her integrity meant everything. Although she always handled the truth with kindness, she refused to sugarcoat. Not that her tactfulness made running into the recipient of a bad review any less uncomfortable.

He seemed to take her silence as another slight. "You'll have to excuse me, ladies. I was just about to go on break."

He set a sign on the table that read *Help yourself to a free sample*, and headed for the wooden steps that led down to the beach.

"What was that all about?" Abby followed her gaze as Evan disappeared from sight.

"I reviewed his taffy about a year ago. He must've recognized me." He wasn't the first disgruntled customer to look her up on the internet. Usually, they sent nasty emails. She rarely ever ran into them in real life.

"I'm guessing it wasn't favorable?" Abby's compassionate nature echoed in her soft, sympathetic tone.

"Last year, you say?" Verna interrupted, her brow crinkled with concern.

"Yes, why?"

"Oh dear, oh dear," Verna mumbled, shaking her head. "That poor boy."

"Why do you say that?" Nadia squelched the rising urge to defend herself. Some people didn't understand her dedication to candor, favoring the "if you can't say something nice, don't say anything at all" approach. Never mind that mentality would render the entire review ecosystem null and void.

Verna sighed, her gaze fixed on an empty space in the distance, as if peering into the past. "Let's just say, last year, your bad review wasn't the worst thing that happened to Evan Blake."

Chapter Four

EVAN

"I DON'T KNOW what came over me, Dad. I lost my cool." Evan Blake dug his fingers through his damp hair, reliving his regrettable reaction at the farmers market.

Storming off like a moody teenager hadn't been his finest moment. But watching Nadia Chopra casually sample his taffy like some first-time tourist hit him like a gut punch. Her review had decimated his fledgling confidence *and* his pride. And the real kicker: she didn't even remember. How's that for an ego boost?

He stopped pacing the cold linoleum floor and turned to face his father. He'd lost even more color than the day before, and dark shadows hung above his high cheekbones like half-moons. The occasional twitch of his papery eyelids served as the only sign of life apart from the rhythmic beep of the heart monitor.

"If Mom were here, she'd make me apologize. She'd say something like 'Rudeness leads a man to ruin.' Or 'Manly men mind their manners.'" He smiled at the silly sayings—she had one for everything. They used to bug him, but now, he'd sit through a thousand of his mother's well-meaning maxims if it meant hearing her voice again.

His gaze drifted to the bouquet of daisies decorating the side table—yellow, his mother's favorite. She called them little stems of sunshine. Which is probably why Bonnie, his mother's best friend, chose them to brighten his father's hospital room. Although, he never understood why people gave get-well flowers. What ailing person wanted to watch something beautiful shrivel and die? Did they really need another reminder that nothing good in life would last?

Turning his back on the bittersweet blooms, he inched closer to his father's bedside. When had he become so frail? Youthful and active, his dad had always kept himself in good shape, either surfing or running the shoreline every morning. But this past year, he hadn't stepped foot on the beach, and it showed. No longer tanned and toned, he looked older than his sixty-five years.

Only three days had passed since the stroke that brought him to Blessed Heart Hospital, but his father had started slipping away long before that.

"Hey, Dad?" Evan reached for his hand, but stopped short, his fingertips resting on the stark white sheets. "When are you coming back?" The words scratched his throat, lingering in the loud silence between them.

The doctors had tried to explain all the medical jargon to help him understand how a stroke can cause a coma, and what causes a stroke in the first place. But Evan didn't need charts and lab results to know what happened. He just needed a calendar.

Three days ago marked the one-year anniversary of his mother's death. And whether or not it made sense, he was convinced his father simply refused to go on without her. Not that he planned to mention his theory aloud.

At the creaking of the door, he whipped his hand back and cleared his throat.

"How's he doing?" Bonnie Larsen breezed into the room, her bright, bubbly aurora illuminating the dull space with some much-needed vibrancy.

"About the same." Evan moved to one of the folding chairs, making room for Bonnie by his father's bedside.

"Michael Stanley Blake," she scolded with playful sternness. "We've had enough of your shenanigans. It's time you haul your stubborn heinie out of bed, you hear me?" She set a box of salted caramel pralines on the table beside the daisies and bent to kiss his forehead.

Evan suppressed a chuckle. She may be only five foot two, but the tiny spitfire could keep a herd of ornery bulls in line. And she'd do it with a smile, too. Despite her petite size, she had the biggest heart of anyone he knew. And when his mother died, she'd helped him keep the business going, letting him operate Tammy's Taffy out of her own Main Street candy shop, Sweet Blessings.

"And how are *you* doing?" She swept her gaze over his still-damp hair, T-shirt, and board shorts.

"Fine."

"Did you go surfing this morning?" Without waiting for an answer, she rumpled his hair, then rubbed her fingers together. "Sticky with salt water. Just as I suspected." She frowned like a disappointed schoolteacher. "You'll catch your death in that icy water! Can't you wait until summer like a sane person?"

"I wear a wet suit."

"Does it cover your head? Because I think you might have frozen some of your brain cells." She clucked her tongue. "And I hope you don't drag Mia out there when she comes to visit. It's bad enough you got her into the hobby when you lived in LA. I already worry about sharks and riptides, I don't need to fret about hypothermia, too."

He laughed. "You know as well as I do that Mia can't be dragged into anything. She makes up her own mind."

"That's true. And I love her for it." She glowed with motherly affection. "Although, I do wish you could've talked her into moving back home with you last year."

"Me, too. It'd be nice to have her around again. Even if it means listening to her tone-deaf Taylor Swift impersonations," he teased. "When's she coming back?"

"Tomorrow. Just in time for the Blessing in a Bottle Festival."

His stomach clenched. Before his mother died, he looked forward to the two-day celebration. Events like Light the Night and the Timber Ball brought the entire town together. But this year...

Dread doused any hint of excitement.

Bonnie must've noticed because her features softened. "Are you worried about the Bitesize Blessing competition?"

He didn't respond, but he didn't need to—his answer was splashed across his face. He'd been working on a new taffy flavor for months, something to compete with the dozens of sweet and savory treats vying for the blue ribbon. The blue ribbon that served as a stamp of approval. Of excellence. But nothing he concocted was good enough. He needed a lightning strike of inspiration. Or more accurately, a miracle.

When it came to taffy, flavor innovation didn't come naturally. Not like surfing, which felt as second nature as intaking oxygen. His mom had been the real confectioner of the family. He could follow a recipe easily enough, but create from scratch? That wasn't his specialty. But he'd have to step up his game if he wanted to win. And he *needed* to win.

"Don't put so much pressure on yourself, sweetheart." She placed a gentle hand on his shoulder. "Win or lose, I know your mother would be proud of you."

Evan nodded, although he didn't share her conviction. Losing the competition wasn't an option. And yet, he had no idea which taffy flavor to enter. And he was running out of time.

His thoughts flew to Nadia Chopra, fixating on her perfect lips as she popped the sample of Madagascar Vanilla into her mouth. She had the kind of soft, supple lips a guy could sink into, and he hated that he'd noticed.

Of course, he wasn't surprised by her beauty. He'd glimpsed photos online when he'd researched her review service last year. Not only did her opinion as a professional reviewer carry serious weight with consumers, she looked like the sort of model who could sell sand to a beach bum.

But photos could be altered and manipulated. As a former prop master in Hollywood, he knew many A-list celebrities who didn't live up to the hype of the big screen in real life. But Nadia? Her glossy black hair, dark, penetrating eyes, and those seductive curves—he shook his head, dismissing the image of her killer figure in the formfitting dress. He didn't care to admit she looked even better in person. In fact, it irked him.

No alluring pout or seductive batting of eyelashes—no

matter how long and thick—could erase her words. Words he couldn't bury in an envelope in the bottom desk drawer because they lived on the internet for all of eternity.

And now, when he needed to focus more than ever before, as the clock counted down to the festival in four days, he couldn't shake her choke hold on his psyche.

He could only hope Nadia Chopra wouldn't be sticking around town for long.

Chapter Five

NADIA

"HOW LONG ARE YOU STAYING, DEAR?"

The question came from Verna, but four other women in their late seventies to mid-eighties stared at her from across Abby's sitting room, teacups poised midair as they waited intently for her response.

"Just a few days."

"You're not staying for the Blessing in a Bottle Festival?" Faye Thompson gazed at her in disbelief. Her huge, doe-like eyes looked almost cartoonish magnified behind thick, black-rimmed glasses. Out of the five women who met at Abby's inn for weekly afternoon tea, Faye was the most sweet and soft-spoken. And thanks to the felt bowler hat that sat askew on her shoulder-length gray hair, she appeared slightly eccentric, too. Albeit, in an endearing way.

"I hadn't planned on it."

"Are you single?" Janet Hill asked with unabashed interest, carefully sipping her tea to avoid smudging her expertly applied lipstick. She was the most vivacious of the group, and with her blond curls and taut skin—most likely aided by a skilled stylist and Botox—she struck Nadia as the forever-young type.

"I am." While she could appreciate a woman who spoke her mind, she wasn't sure how her relationship status was relevant to the conversation.

"Then I suggest you attend the festival," Janet quipped in response to her unspoken thought. "The beach will be crawling with available men."

Gail Lewis snorted and rolled her eyes. "Not every single female is on the hunt for a husband, Janet." She plucked a lemon-glazed sugar cookie from the tiered dessert platter even though she'd already had three. Brusque and no-nonsense, the retired history teacher and girls' high school basketball coach balanced Janet's flashy sensationalism and Faye's warm-and-fuzzy sentimentality. Sensing a kinship, Nadia liked Gail immediately. Even if her fashion choices consisted of a poorly fitted beige pantsuit and clunky leather loafers.

"Who said husband?" Janet retorted with a flip of her hair. "Some company. A good meal. Dancing. Maybe a few diamonds—"

"Conflict-free diamonds," Shirley Milton interjected. She scooped a heaping spoonful of syrupy honey from a mason jar and swirled it into her pungent ginger tea before offering the natural sweetener to Verna, who sat beside her on the sofa. Verna politely declined, and Shirley stuffed the jar back into her patchwork purse.

Although her wardrobe was still stuck in the sixties, Nadia admired Shirley's confidence and commitment to her convictions. She clearly cared deeply for the world around her, and she wasn't a bit fazed by her friend's good-natured teasing.

"Of course," Janet assured her with a smile. "Conflict-free diamonds. And organic opals. And free-range rubies."

Gail snorted again, this time spraying sugar cookie crumbs down her starched white blouse.

Nadia hid a grin behind the rim of her teacup. She'd known the ladies for less than thirty minutes, but she already adored each one of them. Their easy, playful banter spoke of their lifelong friendship, and she hoped she and Abby would share a similar bond when they reached that age.

Before disappearing back into the kitchen to work on her elusive recipe, Abby had introduced the women as the Belles, a social group that functioned as an informal book club and charitable organization. According to Abby, what began as a simple book club in the early 1900s, dedicated to reading *belles-lettres*—a French term for fine and beautiful writing—grew to a group of women who engaged in acts of service around town. Now, the current generation of members had a hand in everything from hosting fundraisers, to bringing meals to the sick, to aiding new mothers with childcare, cooking, and housework. Basically, they were quirky, eclectic, literature-loving angels.

"You know who'd make a nice beau?" Faye asked thoughtfully, nibbling on a raspberry scone. "Michael's boy."

"Ooh-la-la! Evan from Heaven." Janet fanned herself with the linen napkin previously draped in her lap. "He's a dish."

"He's also young enough to be your grandson," Gail reminded her with pointed disapproval.

"Yes, but he isn't *my* grandson, is he?"

While Janet continued to sing Evan's praises, Nadia noticed Verna glance in her direction. Would she mention their awkward exchange at the farmers market earlier that morning?

"I sure hope he wins the Bitesize Blessing competition this year," Shirley said between mouthfuls of her homemade granola bar. Flaxseed and quinoa crumbs peppered her paisley peasant skirt. "He could use some good luck."

Nadia ignored the tiny flutter of guilt swirling in her stomach and asked, "What's the Bitesize Blessing competition?"

"It's an annual contest held during the festival this coming weekend," Verna explained. "Entries can be sweet or savory, but they have to be bitesize."

"Evan's entering taffy in honor of his mother," Faye added. Then, leaning forward, she whispered reverently, "She passed away right before the festival last year."

"In her sixties!" Janet pressed a hand to her chest as if still shaken by the news. "She was practically a baby."

"That's awful." Nadia set her teacup on the coffee table, her thoughts swirling. If she'd known about Evan's situation, would she have changed her review? The answer sprang to mind instantly. No. She couldn't let outside circumstances sway the truth. And yet, something about it still didn't sit right with her soul. As if there was a missing piece in her review process. This wasn't the first time she'd given someone an unfavorable critique and carried a niggling desire to help them fix the problem. But product reinvention wasn't her job.

"She had an embolism." Gail gave a regretful shake of her head. "No one saw it coming."

"That's why we should all take daily supplements." Shirley's tone gave Nadia the impression it wasn't the first time she'd offered the advice. "Rhodiola, reishi, gotu kola, and jiaogulan, for starters."

"Okay, now you're making up words. That sounds like gibberish to me." Janet frowned, then immediately relaxed her facial muscles as if the brief blunder had already added new wrinkles.

"Oh! And garlic pills." Shirley dug inside her purse and produced a small silver tin. "Want one?" She flipped open the lid and the potent aroma flooded the room.

"Good grief, Shirley! Put that away!" Janet wheezed, pinching her nose. "That's pungent enough to kill vampires all the way in Romania."

"Is it that bad?" Shirley shrugged, snapping it closed. "I can barely smell it."

"That's because you're desensitized, dear. To garlic and patchouli." Verna patted her hand kindly.

"The harsh reality is that it doesn't always matter how healthy you are," Gail said frankly. "Look at Michael. Fit as a fiddle. Then a stroke strikes, just like that." She snapped her fingers, startling Faye, who yelped and spilled her tea. "Sorry, Faye."

"That's okay." Faye dabbed her floral brocade vest with her napkin. "Death takes most of us by surprise. That's why it's so important to savor every moment, don't you think?"

"Seize the day, like the Romans say," Janet agreed, sounding almost sage until she wiggled her eyebrows, adding, "And they knew how to *carpe diem*."

She segued into a nostalgic tale about a toga party she attended in the late seventies, but Nadia didn't hear a word. She couldn't stop thinking about Evan and his parents. How devastating to lose one parent and be so close to losing another. Her heart ached for his loss. So much could change so quickly. Not a single second was guaranteed. And time wasn't a commodity that should be squandered.

Her chest tightened.

Three years.... That's how much of her life—and heart—she'd wasted on Brian. And after three long years of her love and loyalty, how had it ended?

She squeezed her eyes shut, blocking out the memory.

The past was the past; she couldn't change it. But tomorrow morning, she'd open her inbox to find an email from her aunt, right on schedule. And, as promised, the email would contain three matches—three men who satisfied her extensive list of carefully curated criteria. And one of those men would be her future spouse. A man she could count on *'til death do us part.*

Nadia opened her eyes, breathing a little easier.

She didn't need sparks, she needed certainty.

And that's exactly what her aunt would provide. She simply needed to sit back, relax, and leave the process in the skilled hands of a professional.

Chapter Six

LOGAN

"RELAX. I'M A PROFESSIONAL."

Dr. Paulson's words did little to assuage Logan Mathews's apprehension as the sharp needle pierced his shoulder, making his muscle twitch.

"Sure. Relax. Never mind that I'm a human pincushion," Logan muttered. Sitting shirtless on a burlap beanbag chair listening to whale mating calls made him uncomfortable enough. Adding needles elevated the experience to cruel and unusual punishment.

"It's not so bad," Dr. Paulson said cheerfully. The guy was nice enough, and good at his job, but his incessantly chipper attitude grated on Logan's nerves. "Once you get used to it, you won't even notice them anymore. Here. I'll show you."

Logan gawked as the man stabbed a needle into his right cheek without batting an eye. "See?" Dr. Paulson said with a smile, eerily nonplussed. "I barely felt a thing. Here. I'll show you again—"

"I'm good," Logan interjected before the horror show

could continue. "I suddenly feel completely relaxed." In truth, he'd never felt more tense in his life. Especially since Dr. Paulson left the needle sticking out of his face and resumed his treatment looking like a life-size voodoo doll.

"So, Doc. You think this'll work?" Logan asked between gritted teeth.

Do not flinch. Do not flinch. Do not flinch.

"In conjunction with deep tissue work and electrotherapy, I think we have a good shot at making some improvement."

Improvement? Logan groaned internally. He knew he shouldn't expect a miracle. He'd been dealing with sporadic muscle spasms for years, ever since his spinal injury. Heck, the fact that he could walk was a miracle in itself. He should be grateful. But still, he'd hoped Dr. Paulson's, let's say, *creative* methods would garner more definitive results. Hence the weekly hour-long bus ride to Torture Town.

After several weeks with zero change, and one of his worst spasms in recent months, Dr. Paulson modified his treatment plan. *Again.* To his credit, the guy didn't give up easily.

"Improvement. That'd be great." Logan tried to sound positive, even as disappointment roiled in his stomach. When he'd started treatment a few months ago, he'd set a personal goal to get his driver's license back in six months. Before Abby and Max, he didn't mind his lack of mobility. Sure, he hated to see his fully remodeled 1972 Chevy El Camino languishing in the garage, but not enough to risk a spasm-induced accident. Besides, until recently, he rarely left the house.

Now, he had a myriad of reasons to regain his independence. But he wouldn't renew unless he'd been spasm free for at least three months. So, doing the math, he didn't stand a chance. Frustration built in his chest, crowding out his lungs.

"You're clenching again," Dr. Paulson pointed out kindly. "Do me a favor and take a deep breath, then exhale slowly."

Logan followed orders, and some of the tension drained from his muscles. He thought about asking the doc to trade in the whale calls for some Motown but decided against it. He simply needed to quiet his thoughts and survive the next thirty minutes.

Except every time he tried to relax, his mind wandered to Abby. And their kiss.

Hands down, that had been the best moment of his life. And he'd thought it marked the start of something great— something groundbreaking. But practically overnight, they'd become parents, and Abby dove headfirst into innkeeping, researching, planning, prepping—he'd never seen her stretched so thin. He'd also never seen her so driven. She took on the role of mother and entrepreneur with all the grit and tenacity of a fighter pilot whose life depended on laser focus.

While he found her determination distractingly enticing —along with everything else about her—it left him in a quandary. How could he pull her attention from Max and the inn for such a selfish reason like going on an actual date? She barely had time for a shower let alone a sunset stroll along the beach.

As much as it pained him—he physically ached for another chance to hold her in his arms—he decided to put a pin in their romantic relationship. Admittedly, not the best choice of words, given the circumstances.

For now, he'd divert every effort into supporting Abby in any way he could. Together, they'd make her dream of owning an award-worthy inn a reality. And they'd give Max the loving family life he deserved.

Even as he recited his well-rehearsed internal monologue, recounting all the reasons their happily ever after could wait, he couldn't ignore the stabs of self-reproof. Or the *literal* stabs as Doc Paulson practiced his needlepoint skills on the back of his neck.

Deep down, he harbored another motivation for pushing the pause button. And it was the same rationale that kept him from telling Abby about his weekly doctor's appointment.

He wanted to come to her as a whole man, without his injury plaguing him at every turn. He wanted to cure his spasms first. And he didn't want to give her false hope in case the treatments didn't work.

A whole lotta *wants* that had more to do with his pride than anything else. And he didn't particularly like what that said about him.

The melancholy thoughts whirred in his mind throughout the rest of his appointment, then during the bus ride back to Blessings Bay, where he picked up Max after soccer practice.

Max sat waiting for him on the lawn in front of the school—a school that boasted a better ocean view than some seaside resorts. It sat high on a bluff, overlooking the bay, and between the crisp, salty air, wild call of the waves, and the sweet scent of freedom, Logan didn't know how the kids—or teachers—got anything done.

"Hey, Maximilian. How was practice?"

"Great!" Max scrambled off the ground and grabbed his backpack. "I scored a goal!"

"That's awesome! Did Coach Keller take you off defense?"

"Just for today. He made everyone switch positions. He said he wanted us to run a mile in someone else's cleats, or something like that. Said it would make us better team players."

"Sounds like your coach knows his stuff." Logan took the street side of the curb as they walked downhill toward home.

"Yeah. He's pretty smart, I guess. He helped me score my goal."

"Oh, yeah? How'd he do that?"

"I kinda froze in the offensive zone. He said to take the shot or pass the ball. I didn't wanna pass, so I took the shot."

"That's good advice." The words circled in Logan's mind on the walk home.

Take the shot or pass the ball.

He didn't want to pass the ball, either. Not when it came to Abby.

Could he find a way to pursue her without hindering her personal goals and upsetting the precarious balancing act they called daily life? It was worth a shot, wasn't it?

His steps grew quicker, propelled by reckless resolve.

He didn't know how they'd make it work, or when they'd find time, or if it would blow up in their faces, but the thought of losing Abby had given him the kick he'd needed. As soon as they got home, he'd ask her on a proper date. They'd iron out the details later.

As they turned down their street, the high-pitched

screech of an alarm stopped Logan in his tracks. His adrenaline spiked.

Smoke spilled from a kitchen window. *Their* kitchen window.

Nadia paced the front lawn with Verna and the other Belles, whipping her head around frantically, searching the shell-shocked faces. "Where's Abby?"

Cold fear gripped him.

"Stay here." Logan left Max in the neighbor's yard and broke into a sprint, praying he wasn't too late.

Chapter Seven

ABBY

ABBY SWATTED THE AIR, attempting to clear the heavy blanket of smoke as another coughing fit shook her frame. The suffocating fumes had flooded the kitchen quicker than she'd anticipated. Once she realized the timer for her French toast casserole hadn't gone off, acrid smoke tendrils already curled from the oven, collecting in a voluminous cloud. She'd only made things worse when she'd thrown open the oven door to retrieve the scorched dish. And dousing the block of charcoal with cold water? Well, that had sent the smoke alarm into full DEFCON 1 mode. Based on its melodramatic wailing, you'd think the entire neighborhood was about to implode.

"Abby!" Logan's muffled cry broke through the thick gray veil surrounding her.

She opened her mouth to respond, but the smoke triggered another cough.

In a matter of seconds, Logan appeared in the fog and scooped her into his arms. She clung to his neck, not about to argue when she'd fantasized about a similar scenario countless times. Only, in her daydreams, she hadn't almost burned the house down.

Without a word, he carried her outside into the crisp, clean air.

Nadia, Max, and the Belles huddled on the lawn, their tense expressions awash with relief when they spotted her.

"Oh, thank goodness!" Nadia breathed. "When I noticed you were still inside—"

"I'm fine," Abby assured her, blushing as she realized Logan still hadn't set her down.

"Are you sure?" His eyes peered into hers.

"Uh-huh," she murmured, acutely aware of his hands around her waist and thighs. Why hadn't he put her down yet? And why didn't she want him to?

"She looks fine to me," Janet teased, bringing the rest of the world back into focus.

Abby's blush deepened, and Logan cleared his throat, regrettably lowering her to the ground.

As soon as her feet touched the front porch, Max scrambled up the steps and flung his arms around her. "I wanted to go in and rescue you, but Logan said I had to wait outside."

"I'm so glad you listened." She gave Max a squeeze. "Although, thankfully, it wasn't an actual fire."

"What happened?" Faye stared wide-eyed as smoke curled from the crack in the kitchen window.

Thanks to the old, warped frame, Abby hadn't been able to open it more than a few inches.

"I, uh, burnt a breakfast casserole," she admitted sheepishly.

To her surprise, Logan chuckled.

"And why is that funny?" she demanded.

"Let's just say, I had a similar experience the first time I tried to cook for you." He met her gaze again, and the warm glimmer of affection in his beautiful blue eyes made the ground sway beneath her feet.

That night in December, when she'd returned home from her soul-searching stroll through town, famished and too tired to cook, she'd found dinner already on the table. Logan's kindness that evening had stirred something in her heart—a fondness and appreciation that had only grown deeper and more impossible to ignore.

"As much as I'm enjoying this tender trip down memory lane," Gail cut in brusquely, "can we do something about that incessant alarm?"

Abby blinked, returning to the present. She'd been so distracted by her reverie she must've tuned out the noise.

"I'll take care of it. Along with the smoke." Logan ducked back inside, and Abby immediately missed his presence.

The brief moment she'd spent in his arms—close, cradled, and cared for—had simultaneously sparked and satisfied a longing she'd been trying to squelch for months. She wanted more of Logan. More than shared glances across a room. More than scattered sentences and a fleeting connection. So much more than time and circumstances would allow.

She contemplated following him inside and announcing right then and there, amid the suffocating smoke, that they needed to make this—*them*—work, whatever the cost.

Bingley's sharp, agitated bark broke through her thoughts, and Abby turned to find chaos unfurling on her front lawn.

A large lop-eared rabbit darted from the bushes, bounding straight toward the Belles. Startled, Faye and Janet yelped and scattered in opposite directions while Shirley dropped to her knees, flinging her arms wide in welcome.

The bunny, disinterested in being caught, doubled back, much to Bingley's delight. He barked in excitement, which sent their uninvited guest into another sprint, and a rousing game of Catch the Rabbit ensued.

Abby watched in dumbstruck amusement as Gail, summoning her high school coaching skills, shouted orders to her ragtag team of rabbit wranglers. The women formed a large circle on the lawn to corral the rascally renegade, while Bing, Max, and Bugs Bunny zigzagged back and forth in the center.

Accompanied by the smoke and screeching alarm, the whole scene would've been absurdly entertaining, were it not for the familiar vehicle turning onto State Street, heading straight toward them.

Panic vaulted into Abby's throat.

This can't be happening. Not today. Not now.

The bright-teal 1975 VW Bus cautiously eased into her driveway.

No, no, no... please, no!

Abby tried to will the driver's door shut with her mind, but it slowly creaked open.

Serena Scott—aka the Savvy Sojourner—slid from the driver's seat and into the bedlam. With wary, narrowed eyes, the pretty, polished, eternally camera-ready blonde swept her gaze from the one-ring circus to the cloud of smoke billowing from the window Logan had managed to open wider, thus releasing an even bigger plume.

Abby groaned as her heart sank alongside her hopes and dreams.

To make the already appalling situation even worse, a faded red fire truck—clearly a holdover from the '50s or '60s—careened down their street, sirens wailing. Well, more like *sputtering*.

It lurched to a stop, and a young, freckle-faced firefighter leaped to the ground. "Is this 1109 West State Street?"

"I sure hope not," Serena muttered loud enough for Abby to hear.

She winced, swallowing the bitter taste of dread and disappointment as she addressed the firefighter's question. "It is. I'm sorry you had to come out, but there's no fire. Only smoke from a burnt casserole."

At that exact moment, Logan succeeded in quieting the alarm, giving way to an uncomfortable silence.

"Darn." The young man's face fell, as if he hadn't witnessed much excitement in his brief career. "Well, I guess we'll be off, then." He turned and shouted to the older driver, "False alarm, Joe. You can go back to your knitting."

"I'm making a beer cozy," Joe called out the window, as if he needed to defend his hobby.

"Thanks for stopping by." Abby thought about asking them to stay in case she keeled over from the embarrassment of facing Serena and needed CPR. Or a defibrillator. Of all the possible moments for the travel blogger to arrive, why this one? And why days early?

She gathered a fortifying breath and forced a smile as the fire truck executed a twenty-point turn in the street, accidentally nudging Verna's mailbox in the process. Heaven forbid they ever encountered a real emergency.

"Welcome to Blessings on State Street," she said with as much sincerity as she could muster. "You must be Serena."

"I was hoping my GPS had led me to the wrong place." Serena's delicate nose scrunched in obvious disgust as she observed the maelstrom on the front lawn.

Nadia had finally wrangled Bing, who continued to bark as Max cornered the bunny at the base of the oak tree. The Belles, on the other hand, had abandoned the rescue attempt in favor of rubbernecking the trainwreck—aka Abby's hopes for a rave review going up in smoke along with her casserole.

Stay calm. Stay professional. She kept her smile glued in place. "We weren't expecting you for a few more days."

"Then you made a mistake. My reservation is for today."

Serena's curt tone poked the feeble dam keeping Abby's emotions in check. That couldn't be right. How had she made such a monumental mistake? She was certain she'd scheduled Serena's stay for the coming Friday. But what could she say? They'd already gotten off on the wrong foot. Arguing would only make matters worse. If that was possible.

"Yes, of course. My apologies." She racked her brain for some way to salvage the situation. "You've had a long drive. Why don't we take a stroll around back to the garden? There's a lovely view of the ocean. I can bring out some tea and charcuterie. And once you've had a chance to relax for a bit, I can show you to your room." She was sure she could borrow some things from Verna if the smoke hadn't cleared from the kitchen yet.

"I guess that would be fine."

Serena didn't sound too enthusiastic, but Abby would

take what she could get. Maybe she had a shot at turning things around?

"Abby! Abby!" Max rushed toward them, the rabbit cradled in his arms. "Look! Isn't he cool?"

"He's adorable." Abby conjured another smile for Max's sake, eager to shield him from her own worry and apprehension.

"Can I keep him?"

He looked so hopeful, she hated to disappoint him. But odds were high that the bunny already belonged to someone in their neighborhood. Lop-eared rabbits didn't roam wild. Before she could respond, a loud sneeze drew her attention.

Serena sniffled. "You didn't mention anything about a rabbit. As an innkeeper, you have a duty to notify guests of any animals living on the premises."

Abby bit her tongue. Of course she'd be allergic. She glanced back at Max, who peered up at her with large, expectant eyes, and her chest squeezed.

"We'll talk about this later, okay?" she said softly, then caught Nadia's eye, mouthing a silent *SOS*.

Nadia, who'd inched closer, concern etched in her features, abandoned all pretense of subtlety and hurried over to join them, ready to intercede in any way she could. She'd always been the kind of friend Abby could count on; a trait she appreciated now more than ever.

Their practice drill had just become an all-hands-on-deck emergency, and if Abby had any hope of redeeming her reputation, she'd need all the help she could get.

NADIA

NADIA STRODE across the Main Street promenade, barely registering the pleasant evening breeze or the way it smelled faintly of fried, buttery fish and fresh sourdough.

She couldn't shake the feeling that something wasn't quite right with Abby's new guest, Serena Scott. Sure, reservation mistakes happened. And Abby had been frazzled and overwhelmed lately. But Nadia had a niggling suspicion there was more to the story. Only, she couldn't put her finger on *what*, exactly.

At the end of the promenade, she skipped down the wooden steps leading to the beach—the same steps Evan Blake had retreated down earlier that day. The image of his toned back and shoulders in his tight white T-shirt had been burned into her brain.

Dismissing it from her mind with the sharp reminder that the man couldn't stand her, she ambled onto the beach. Her heels sank into the cool sand, and she slipped off her sandals before heading toward the end of the cove where

Abby said she'd find a small stand selling the freshly caught clams she wanted for dinner that night.

The setting sun cast shades of coral, persimmon, and coppery gold across the water in such an arresting display, Nadia stopped in her tracks, allowing her toes to sink even deeper into the silky granules. A quaint lighthouse winked at her from the tip of the cape, and for a moment, she couldn't move, too transfixed by the beauty before her. She wasn't typically a stop-and-smell-the-roses kind of person, but Blessings Bay had a strange way of inspiring stillness. Reverence, even. And she could find herself getting used to it.

She gazed at the horizon line where the sun dipped beneath the glassy surface. A lone surfer rode high atop a wave, floating free and unencumbered. What would it feel like to soar above the world, so far from shore, with nothing around you but the wild ocean waters? Powerful? Liberating? Absolutely terrifying?

Her imagination conjured a predatory shark, lurking in the shadowy depths, waiting to strike, the poor surfer completely unaware. Her pulse quickened. What would she do if—

A jarring *buzz* vibrated in the pocket of her cardigan, and Nadia jumped, slapping a palm to her racing heart. *Good grief.* It was only her cell phone. Catching her breath, she checked the caller ID.

Ishani Masi.

She pressed the phone to her ear, her gaze fixed on the surfer as he sailed toward the shore—and safety. "Hello."

"I have the best news!" Before Nadia could respond, her aunt gushed, "I know I promised you three matches by tomorrow morning, but, honey, we don't need them. I found

The One. He's perfect. Rich, gorgeous, lives in LA, is from a great family, and, Nadia, I'm not exaggerating when I say you two were made for each other. Practically with the same mold! Your life goals, aspirations, hobbies, likes and dislikes —nearly identical! He even shares your bizarre aversion to pickles!"

"He sounds nice," Nadia murmured, momentarily distracted by the tall figure emerging from the water.

The man's lean, sculpted body glistened in a slick black wet suit that clung to every well-defined inch of him.

"Nice? Honey, he isn't some silk pashmina on sale at Hermès. He's all of Rodeo Drive! And I think you two should meet ASAP. This kind of relationship real estate won't remain on the market long."

"Uh-huh," Nadia muttered, her mouth dry as the scintillating stranger hoisted his surfboard under one arm and strode up the beach, headed straight toward her. Although she'd never seen an episode of *Baywatch*, she had an inkling the hunky cast couldn't compare to this guy's sultry stride.

But as he drew closer, bringing his features into full view, her heart fell, plummeting all the way to her bare feet.

"Fabulous! I'll email you his portfolio and set something up. I can't wait for you to meet him. I guarantee, the second you lay eyes on this one, every other man will cease to exist."

Nadia wasn't sure what she said to her aunt or if she even managed a quick goodbye. She still clutched the phone against her ear as Evan Blake stood two feet away, equally surprised to see her.

"Hey." He ran his fingers through his wet hair, his movements hesitant and oddly endearing.

"Hi." She let the phone slip from her ear, and stuffed it

back into her pocket, shockingly, at a complete loss for words.

They stood for a few minutes facing each other, the awkward silence punctuated by the occasional seagull's cry.

Evan cleared his throat. "I owe you an apology."

Startled by his unexpected admission, Nadia finally found her voice. "No, you don't. I owe *you* one. As soon as you left the farmers market, I figured out the connection. If I'd realized sooner, I never would've—"

"It's all good. I shouldn't have expected you to remember. You probably review thousands of products every year. You can't remember them all. Especially when they're as unremarkable as mine." He flashed a self-deprecating smile, and Nadia winced.

"For what it's worth, I saw potential in your product. And in my review, I did mention several things I liked about it. I was just... hoping for more."

He shrugged. "You're entitled to your opinion."

"My opinion is based on years of experience. Studying industries, markets, and trends, comparing countless products for quality, creativity, and the elusive *je ne sais quoi*. I take hundreds of factors into account. My reviews aren't based on my personal whim." Why did she feel the need to defend herself? She stood by her assessment. And if he really wanted a top-notch product, he shouldn't dismiss her "opinion" so cavalierly.

He studied her for a moment with those intense blue-green eyes.

She shifted her feet in the sand, unnerved by the depth of his gaze.

"You're probably right," he said at last, then pivoted, poised to head down the beach in the opposite direction.

She should let him go. She didn't owe him another word. And yet, she couldn't let the conversation drop. "I can help," she blurted, before the thought had fully formed in her mind.

He glanced over his shoulder, one eyebrow raised. "With what?"

Leave it alone, Nadia. Tell him never mind and let him walk away.

"With the Bitesize Blessing competition," she rambled on, ignoring her own advice. "If you enter one of your current flavors, you won't stand a chance."

He stiffened, propping his surfboard in the sand. "And how do you know that?"

"Because I've judged dozens of contests just like this one. I know what the judges look for. And right now, your taffy doesn't have what it takes to win. That's a fact." Okay, so it wasn't a *fact*. But she'd tasted desserts from CeCe's café, and chocolates from Sweet Blessings, and she knew the competition would be fierce. Unless Evan developed a brand-new flavor—something with originality and panache—he didn't have a shot at the blue ribbon.

A wounded glint flickered in his eyes, and she got the feeling it had nothing to do with his pride. Her thoughts flew to what Faye said about Evan's mother and her legacy. Softening, she added, "I'm sorry if that sounds harsh. I have a tendency to be too blunt sometimes. But I'm genuinely trying to help."

"Why?"

Nadia blinked, taken aback by his question. A question

she couldn't answer. At least, not without further introspection—a habit she'd been trying to avoid lately. "Does it matter? I can help you win. The real question is, do you want my help or not?"

He cocked his head, those piercing eyes looking right through her again. Finally, after what felt like hours, he said, "Meet me at Sweet Blessings tomorrow morning at eight."

And without another word, he turned, lifted his surfboard, and strode down the beach, leaving her to stand alone in stunned silence.

She exhaled a heavy breath as reality settled.

What on earth had she just done?

Chapter Nine

EVAN

"SO, WHAT'S HER NAME?"

Evan ignored the question, maneuvering around the lanky form of Mia Larsen.

She leaned against the stainless steel prep island, oblivious to the fact that she kept getting in his way. Ever since they were kids and their moms would get together and tow them along, she'd stuck to him like a lump of melted taffy glued to his pocket. Although he pretended to be annoyed, he didn't usually mind. He kinda liked having a pseudo little sister. Until they both hit middle school and all his friends became more interested in Mia than hanging out with him. Then, he saw the downside. Not that he blamed Mia. It wasn't her fault her golden blond hair, perpetually sparkling blue eyes, and pretty heart-shaped face turned all the boys into hormonal idiots.

"Do you mind?" He gestured to the counter space occupied by her bony elbows.

"Yes, I do. But since I'm a kind, generous person, I'll

move." She flashed a teasing grin and hopped onto the opposite counter.

"You do realize sitting on the counter isn't sanitary."

"What are you trying to say?" she cried in mock protest. Shifting to one side, she brushed her backside a few times, as if she'd sat on some crumbs, then grinned again. "There. Clean as a whistle. Now, quit changing the subject. Who's the girl?"

"What girl?" He turned his back to her and grabbed one of the ripened bananas from the bowl.

"Whichever girl inspired you to trade in your boring board shorts and T-shirt combo for slacks and a shirt with those flap thingies by your neck."

"You mean a collar?"

Her eyes glowed with a mischievous twinkle. "I was just checking to see if *you* knew what it was called."

"Har-har." Evan rolled his eyes and hid a smile as he peeled the brown-speckled skins. She had him pegged. He wasn't even sure why he owned this shirt, let alone why he'd worn it this morning.

"So, are you going to tell me her name or what?"

Evan sighed. She wasn't going to let up, so he might as well confess. "Her name's Nadia Chopra. And I barely know her."

"Oh, her name sounds fancy. I bet she's sophisticated."

"Why would you assume that? Her name's almost the same as yours, give or take a few letters." He neglected to mention she was spot-on.

"Why, I do declare"—Mia fanned herself like an affronted Southern belle, overacting to comical effect—

"Evan Nathaniel Blake, are you saying I'm not sophisticated?"

He eyed her cutoff shorts, pink Crocs, and baseball cap with *Professional Noisemaker*—a nod to her job as a Foley artist for film and TV—emblazoned across the front with a look that said, *Do you really want me to answer that?*

"Fair enough." She laughed. "And if you must know, the more syllables in the name, the more sophisticated the woman."

"How scientific." He shook his head in amusement, slicing the peeled bananas in preparation for Nadia's arrival. He had no idea what Nadia had in mind for the morning but figured it would be a good idea to walk her through the process, from start to finish, at least once before she worked her so-called magic.

Although he'd never admit it to anyone—he barely wanted to admit it to himself—he'd accepted her offer purely for the chance to see her again. Something about the enigmatic know-it-all intrigued him despite the fact she'd insulted his confectionary skills. Plus, he was a tad curious to see how the sophisticated city girl planned to improve his mother's recipe.

Nadia Chopra exuded the vibe of someone who dined at five-star restaurants every night, not a woman who liked to cook for herself. But he'd also learned outward appearances didn't always reflect the inside. And he had a feeling there might be more to Nadia Chopra than met the eye.

His thoughts flew to their conversation on the beach last night. *I'm genuinely trying to help.* She'd sounded so earnest. And there was something in her eyes—an open, unguarded glimmer—that had taken him by surprise. Every nuance, from her posture to her expression, lent conviction to her words. And he realized, much to his chagrin, that he believed her.

For the past year, he'd carried resentment toward this woman, dumping all his internal fears and doubts on her shoulders. Even then, he knew, deep down, that wasn't fair. But it had felt safe—safer to blame someone he'd never met than confront his own conflicted and confusing emotions. Now that Nadia had become a living, breathing woman—not just some flawless and intimidating image on the internet—he needed to face facts. Somehow, he'd created a life he didn't want. And even worse, he was failing at it—miserably.

"So, how'd you meet?" Mia asked, interrupting his morose thoughts.

"It's a long story."

"Give me the bullet points. Unless you want me to hang around here all day and ask her myself."

"Fine," he relented with a heavy sigh. "About a year ago, when I first took over Mom's business, she reviewed my taffy, didn't like it, and now she's helping me come up with a recipe for the Bitesize Blessing competition."

"Intriguing. And you're okay with that?"

"Yeah, why?" He stopped slicing and shot her a sideways glance.

She shrugged. "I don't know. I guess I'm just surprised. You're always so protective of your mom's taffy. Remember when Mom offered to help?"

Evan turned back to the task at hand, without giving her an answer. Of course he remembered. It was shortly after his mom's death. Bonnie offered to buy the business and absorb it under Sweet Blessings while keeping the name Tammy's Taffy in honor of his mom. A perfect solution, in many respects. And he often wondered if he should've accepted the offer. But at the time, he hadn't wanted to give up that part of his mom—the only piece of her he had left.

He swallowed against the sudden surge of emotion swelling in his throat. "You're right. I don't know what I was thinking when I agreed to this." He let the knife clatter against the cutting board. Did he have time to call Nadia and cancel? As soon as the thought entered his mind, he remembered that he'd never asked for her phone number. *Perfect.*

Mia slid off the counter. "I'm sorry, Ev. I didn't mean to kill the mood." She stood beside him, making him meet her gaze. "Yes, I'm surprised. But that's not a bad thing. I actually think it's great you're letting someone into this part of your life. I know it's been tough." Her eyes shimmered with compassion and empathy, as if she understood all the pain he carried.

Before he could respond, she slipped her arms around his neck, and for the first time in ages, Evan felt himself relax. Mia's hugs had a strange way of communicating without words. When she arrived that morning, her hug had said, *I'm so sorry about your dad. I've been praying for him.* This time, it said, *I'm so happy you met someone. And I'll be praying this one sticks around.*

He didn't have the heart to tell Mia her cheerful optimism couldn't be more misplaced. Not only was Nadia Chopra woefully uninterested in him, she lived several hours away. Plus, they had nothing in common, apart from opposable thumbs and an intrinsic need for oxygen. Not exactly a recipe for happily ever after. So why did a tiny, infinitesimal, microscopic, barely even noticeable part of him want Mia to pray for a happy ending anyway?

A throat cleared, and he looked up from Mia's embrace.

Over her shoulder, he spotted Nadia standing in the doorway, watching them with an unreadable expression.

Chapter Ten

NADIA

AN INEXPLICABLE FLUTTER swam in the pit of Nadia's stomach at the sight of Evan wrapped in the arms of a mysterious woman. The statuesque blonde appeared to be mostly made of legs. Tan, toned legs.

But why should she be surprised? Of course Evan had a beautiful girlfriend. And as of 6:57 that morning, when her aunt's email pinged her inbox, she was well on her way to having the perfect boyfriend. Varun Kumar. Stanford graduate. Successful business broker. And six feet of simmering seduction in a tailored Armani suit. Evan Blake's relationship status didn't matter in the slightest.

Evan stiffened when he spotted her, and Miss Legs slipped her arms from around his neck, turned, and offered her the brightest smile she'd ever seen.

"Hi! You must be Nadia." The woman extended her hand. "I'm Mia."

Nadia tried to match her smile. "It's nice to meet you."

"We were just talking about you." Mia tossed a smirk at

Evan, who looked decidedly uncomfortable. "How long will you be in Blessings Bay?"

"Only a few more days." She'd offered to pack up her things as soon as Serena arrived, but Abby had asked her to stay for moral support. *Poor Abby.* If she'd been frazzled before, she'd practically come unglued during the last twenty-four hours.

Before she'd left that morning, Nadia had found her friend in the kitchen—where she'd been elbow deep in flour since 5 a.m.—baking every recipe in Betty Crocker's arsenal. She'd volunteered to postpone her appointment with Evan in order to help out, but Abby insisted she baked better alone. And considering she could barely find her way to the coffee maker amid Abby's ordered chaos, Nadia was inclined to agree. She'd promised to be back by late morning so they could take Serena to CeCe's for coffee and a craft class.

"Only a few days?" Mia echoed with genuine disappointment. "That's a shame. But you'll be here for the Blessing in a Bottle Festival this weekend?"

"I hadn't planned on staying that long."

"Then you should change your plans! You have to be here for the Timber Ball. Please, say you'll stay."

"I'll think about it," Nadia offered noncommittally, confused by the woman's enthusiastic insistence. Why did she care whether she stayed or not?

"Excellent! I'll take that as a yes." Mia clapped her hands. "My work here is done. You kids have fun." She shot Evan another grin before enveloping Nadia in a warm hug as if they'd been friends for years. "It was so nice to meet you. We should get together again before you leave." With a final wave, she flounced through the swinging door that led to the shop floor.

"Wow," Nadia breathed, staring after her with a mixture of awe and envy. The woman radiated joy, as if she possessed an endless supply. "Is she always that energetic and chipper?"

"Pretty much. She's been like that since we were kids. We used to call her the Energizer Bunny because she never seemed to slow down. And based on her choice of Halloween costume for several years running, I don't think she minded the nickname." He chuckled at the memory, and she liked the way it softened his features. Since they'd met, he'd mostly worn a scowl—and it had been mostly aimed at her.

"You two grew up together?"

"Yeah, our moms were best friends. Mia's like a sister to me."

Nadia found herself smiling, but she wasn't sure why. Girlfriend or sister—what difference did it make?

"Here. You might want to wear this." He handed her a floral apron with *Sweet Blessings* embroidered on the front in a pretty cursive font.

"Thanks." She looped it over her head, careful not to disturb her ponytail. It had taken her a lot longer than she'd anticipated to achieve a simple ponytail that looked sleek, not sloppy.

"I figured I'd walk you through the process, then you could put your magic spin on it."

"Sounds good." She forced a confident smile. Magic? She may have set the bar a little too high during her speech last night. She still had no clue how she'd improve Evan's taffy, only that it needed *something*. She suspected Evan—like so many other entrepreneurs she'd met—had become too close to his creation to think outside the box. Sometimes, it took a fresh perspective to see what was missing. After years of reviewing everything from sunscreen to socks, she had an eye for products; a knack for knowing what would sell and what wouldn't. And with any luck, a brilliant idea would strike while she watched Evan work.

As Evan walked her through the first few steps, Nadia barely spoke a word, too enthralled by his deft, fluid movements. The man had serious skill. More so than she'd realized.

After he carefully weighed and measured each ingredient, he added them to a large copper pot, then heated the mixture over the stove until it reached the very precise temperature of 249 degrees, stirring constantly. When he added the ripened banana, the entire kitchen brimmed with the sweet, caramelized scent of freshly baked banana bread.

Nadia's mouth watered. His flavor offerings may be prosaic, but she couldn't deny the superior quality. Or the fact that he performed most of the steps by hand. "Aren't there machines that will do the work for you?"

"Yeah, but I like doing it this way. It's how my mom always did it."

Her heart tugged at the softness in his voice when he spoke about his mother. He'd clearly loved her dearly. Enough to take over her business and devote himself to making taffy—a career that didn't appear to be his deepest passion, and yet, he'd dedicated his heart and soul to it anyway.

He hefted the huge copper pot from the stove and poured the thick, sweetly scented syrup onto a long metal table, sending another heady whiff of banana bread into the air. "This is the cooling table. It's filled with cold water and helps lower the temperature of the taffy, transforming it from this syrupy consistency to something soft and pliable, ready to be pulled—my favorite part of the process."

He spread the aromatic mixture across the chilled surface and handed her a small wooden bowl filled with coarse sea salt. "Now, we sprinkle this over the top, then fold it into the taffy as it cools."

Nadia pinched the granules between her fingertips and followed Evan's lead. "This reminds me of making naan with my mom and sisters. I always get the job of sprinkling the bread with sea salt and parsley right before serving."

"You cook?"

"Not as often as I used to. But my mom made sure each of her daughters could make every family recipe with their eyes closed. And, of course, a perfect cup of chai."

He cast her a sideways glance, almost as if he was seeing her in a whole new light. And was it her imagination or did he seem to like what he saw?

"I've had chai a few times. It's pretty good."

"If you only think it's *pretty* good, then you've never had authentic chai," she said with a smile.

"Is that so?" He raised both eyebrows, matching her teasing tone. She liked this playful side of him.

"My mom makes her own spice blend, grinding fresh spices she buys back home in India. Most coffee shops and restaurants in the States use chai concentrate or artificially flavored syrup."

Evan grimaced. "Sounds like a lot of confectioners I know. Sure, the good ingredients cost more, but it's worth it. My mom used to say, use the best and ditch the rest."

"Mine has a similar philosophy. Once, she came over for dinner when I was in college and caught me using jarred tikka masala sauce. She nearly fainted." At the memory, a laugh bubbled to the surface.

"That's nothing." Evan flashed a challenging—and unbelievably charming—grin. "One Halloween, my mom caught me handing out mini candy bars to trick-or-treaters. She was so appalled, she dragged me into the kitchen and started making a batch of taffy right there on the spot."

"She didn't." Nadia snickered in disbelief.

"Not only that, but for the next hour, trick-or-treaters piled into my tiny kitchen to watch her make it and take turns pulling the taffy."

Nadia laughed until tears filled her eyes as Evan painted a picture of that night—his mother dressed as the Wicked Witch, stirring a pot on the stove like a cauldron while little ghouls and goblins got gooey taffy all over his floor and furniture as he stress-ate an entire bag of chocolate on the couch.

"Needless to say," he concluded, "I've passed out homemade taffy every Halloween since then."

"I'm sure your mother would be very proud," she said without thinking. As soon as the words left her mouth, a spark of sadness flickered in his eyes. "I'm so sorry," she added quickly, awash with empathy. "I didn't mean to—"

"It's okay. I kinda like talking about her with you."

He met her gaze, and an unspoken connection passed between them like an invisible current, drawing them closer together. She wanted to know more, to ask about both his parents. Was his father still in the hospital? What did the doctors say? Would he be all right? She hadn't known Evan long, and yet, she found herself deeply invested in the cares of his heart. She chalked it up to casual concern and friendly compassion, but was it something more?

For a moment, they stood perfectly still, neither one looking away. Then suddenly, Evan cleared his throat, snapping the metaphorical door shut.

She dismissed the unsettling sting of disappointment, determined to distance herself. What happened in Evan's personal life wasn't any of her business.

"Ready to pull some taffy?" He hefted the mound of candy off the table.

"By hand?"

"Yep." He hoisted the heavy, dense lump over a silver hook hanging on the wall.

The candy sagged under its own weight, smooth and malleable, like a ball of warm candle wax, only on a much larger scale. Evan tugged the taffy toward the ground, twisting and stretching it only to loop it back over the hook, repeating the process, again and again.

Nadia tried to concentrate on his movements rather than dwell on the strange swish in her stomach when he'd held her gaze. But something about the way his muscular forearms flexed from the exertion only made the internal Tilt-A-Whirl worse.

"Ready to give it a try?" Without waiting for a reply, he stepped to the side, making room in front of the hook.

As he passed her the taffy, it sank in her grip like a bucket of lead. "Oof," she grunted. "It's even heavier than it looks." She clumsily mimicked his pulling technique, struggling to lift it back onto the hook.

"Here. I'll help." He stood behind her, so close she smelled the lingering scent of salt water on his skin. His strong arms circled around her, and his large, rough hands rested on top of hers, guiding her movements. Tucked into the curve of his body, every sensation heightened tenfold. How was it possible to feel both safe and dangerously on edge?

It's a perfunctory biological reaction. It doesn't mean anything. Focus, Nadia. Pull, stretch, twist, loop. Rinse and repeat.

"The pulling process aerates the taffy, giving it the soft, chewy texture." Evan's voice sounded lower than usual, rougher, almost husky, as if he, too, found it difficult to breathe.

Nadia inhaled sharply, trying to concentrate on anything other than the heat from Evan's body or the way his chin occasionally grazed the top of her head. She focused her thoughts on the rich, pleasant aroma of banana bread. The warm notes of caramel and cream would taste wonderful with a cup of hot chai. She conjured notes of cinnamon, cardamom, and ginger, but the distraction didn't last.

As soon as Evan said her name, her heart stopped, plummeting to the floor. "Uh-huh?" she mumbled, not trusting her own voice.

"I was wondering—"

Evan hesitated, and she dared to glance over her shoulder. When their eyes met, a zing of electricity shot through her, leaving her mouth dry. The question lingered on his lips, but did she want to hear it? The intensity of his gaze—and the way he leaned a fraction of an inch closer—filled her with apprehension. A physical spark meant nothing. She could achieve the same result shuffling her stockinged feet across a shag carpet.

Chemistry could be cultivated. But compatibility? That took precedence over everything else. It had to. And no matter how good the man looked in a wet suit, or how sweet his taffy tasted, Evan Blake wasn't a match. Varun Kumar, on the other hand, couldn't be more perfect. He deserved her complete and undivided attention.

She'd help Evan win the competition, then they'd go their separate ways.

Evan opened his mouth to speak, but before he got a word out, Nadia blurted, "I know what flavor you should enter in the competition."

ABBY

ABBY STARED at the bright-blue door of the bungalow. She'd been inside before. This wasn't anything new. Besides, Logan had given her permission. And yet, she couldn't bring herself to reach for the doorknob.

Something about stepping inside Logan's space—his *home*—in his absence felt too personal. Too intimate. Without his watchful gaze, she'd be tempted to search for signs in the lingering impression on his pillow, the stack of books on his nightstand, or the way he arranged his furniture. Even the tiniest of details would become a clue—a peek into his complicated and frustratingly confusing mind.

Don't overthink it, Abby. You're just checking on Ron.

Squaring her shoulders, she stepped inside the modest space. The bungalow's typical scent of salty ocean air mixed with minty menthol from Logan's pain relief ointment now offered another, more earthy aroma—hay and rabbit food pellets.

They'd decided to let Max keep the lop-eared bunny—unless they located the rabbit's rightful owners—under one condition: Ron the Rabbit had to temporarily live in the bungalow with Logan, due to Serena's allergies. Max had been thrilled and immediately named the bunny after one of his favorite soccer players, Cristiano Ronaldo. He'd also volunteered to feed Ron and clean up after him. Abby's only role in rabbit-rearing was to check on Ron while Max was at school.

"Hey there, Ron. How's it going?" She knelt in front of the unfinished hutch Logan and Max had started building together last night and unlatched the gate.

Ron gazed up at her with dark, trusting eyes.

"I'm going to let you out to stretch your legs, but don't get into trouble, okay?"

Ron wiggled his nose in agreement and hopped toward her.

Abby scooped him into her arms, gave him a gentle nuzzle, then set him on the ground. "Go explore, and report back if you find anything interesting." She laughed softly, amused as Ron bounded off toward the pile of magazines by Logan's bed as if he understood his mission.

Abby sat cross-legged on the floor and folded her hands in her lap. Then she unfolded them. Then folded them again. When would Logan get back from the hardware store? He'd already been gone an hour. How long did it take to buy materials to fix a leaky faucet?

She kept her gaze glued on Ron—who was now trying to crawl inside one of Logan's work boots—and ignored the cozy reading nook Logan had created in the corner with a worn, comfy armchair and antique lamp. She also ignored the sweet framed photograph of his grandparents on his nightstand—the ones who raised him after his parents died.

And the sagging potted iris Logan was lovingly nursing back to health.

She had a million reasons to fall for Logan Mathews. She didn't need one more. Especially when she wasn't certain he still shared her interest.

A loud *rip* caught her attention, and she scrambled to her feet. "No, Ron. That's not a snack." She grabbed the magazine before he had a chance to nibble another page. "Let's move these out of reach, shall we?" As she gathered the mound in her arms, she expected to see glossy images of military airplanes, vintage cars, or perhaps even gardening. But staring up at her from the top of the bundle was an old issue of *Bed & Breakfast Magazine*.

Her heart fluttered, and she checked the cover underneath.

Bed & Breakfast: Summer 2019: Volume 1: Issue 4

Tears stung her eyes as she scanned article titles like "Best Summer Destinations" and "15 Inns Along the California Coast." Each and every magazine in the stack offered more of the same.

"Oh, Ron," she whispered. "Do you know what this means?"

Ron wiggled his fluffy little tail as if he understood completely.

Logan had been researching all things innkeeping. To help make *her* dream a reality. No one had ever done that before. Even Donnie, who had loved her dearly, had been content for her to follow *his* dreams, not her own. He'd never once asked if she longed for anything other than ghostwriting cookbooks. And when he knew the one thing she wanted most in the world was to be a mother, he couldn't face his own infertility to even discuss other options with her.

A wave of grief and guilt lurched in her stomach. It wasn't fair to compare. They were both incredible men who had trouble talking about their emotions. But the magazines had to mean *something*, didn't they?

"What do you think, Ron? Does this mean Logan still has feelings for me?"

At the creaking of rusty hinges, Abby's heart stopped beating.

Oh, no. Oh, no. Oh, no.

Digging her teeth into her bottom lip, she dragged her gaze toward the telltale sound. Logan stood in the doorway, his expression alarmingly unreadable. How much—if anything—had he heard?

Somehow, she managed to swallow the log of driftwood caught in her throat. "Hey. I was just letting Ron out to stretch his legs and—" Mortified, she realized she was still holding the stack of magazines. Heat seared her skin. "He, uh, thought these were a snack. So, I thought I'd move them." A stuttering mess, she practically tossed them onto the bed like an armed grenade.

Logan glanced at the scattered magazines then met her gaze. "You're here alone?" The huskiness of his voice ignited another rush of heat.

"Except for Ron." *Ugh*. She cringed the second the words toppled off the tip of her tongue. What was wrong with her? She knew what he meant. It was a simple question. And yet, her palms felt slick with sweat and her pulse raced at a dizzying pace.

"Abby." The way he said her name, breathing each

syllable with purpose, weakened her knees, and she was moments away from collapsing onto the mattress with the magazines. He closed the gap between them, an unexpected boldness burning in his eyes. "I've been meaning to ask you something."

She couldn't move. He stood mere centimeters away. The room turned fuzzy.

He was going to kiss her. She felt it vibrating through every inch of her body. Or did she simply want to feel his lips again that desperately?

Logan cleared his throat, inching even closer. "Abby, would you—"

"Hello? Is anyone out here?" Serena's shrill voice echoed across the yard, slicing through their intimate moment without warning or apology.

Abby's hopes clattered to the floor. "I'm so sorry," she mumbled, barely able to breathe, let alone speak.

She was supposed to meet Serena in the foyer at ten. Of all the terrible timing in the world...

"No, it's fine. I get it." He took a step back, clearing her path to the door, their connection broken as a barrier shot up between them. "We don't want to keep the Snobby Sojourner waiting." He softened his words with a half smile, and she tried to match it, but all she felt was crushing disappointment.

Had Logan been seconds away from finally asking her out?

Chapter Twelve

NADIA

NADIA HASTENED DOWN THE SIDEWALK, putting distance between herself and Sweet Blessings—and Evan.

Existing within the intimate bubble of the kitchen— recounting childhood memories, sharing the kind of deep-from-the-belly, close-to-tears laughter born from relatable experiences—had made the invisible tether of electricity between them all the more real and tangible.

If caught soon enough, a spark could be snuffed out. But if you added the tinder of knowledge and connection, of really understanding the person on a deeper level, the spark could ignite into a full-on flame. The kind of flame that could wreak havoc and do untold damage. That was a risk she wasn't willing to take. Not again.

Nadia paused outside CeCe's café and yanked her cell phone from her back pocket.

She'd smother the pesky spark with two texts—one to her aunt, and one to her mother.

She composed the latter first. *Can you send me some of*

your masala blend? Priority overnight. I'll pay the shipping cost.

She didn't go into detail about her plan to make a masala-chai-flavored taffy with Evan for the competition, in case her brilliant idea didn't pan out. But if it did—and she had a strong suspicion it would—she'd be sure to send her parents a box or two as a thank-you. Especially since memories of making masala chai with her mom had been her inspiration.

Almost immediately, her mom texted back. *Of course! Haven't I always said you should keep some handy in your purse?*

Nadia smiled at her mother's thinly veiled I told you so. It was exactly the kind of anecdote she'd shared with Evan that morning. So similar to how Evan's mother always told him to stash a bag of taffy in the glove box of his car in case of "snack emergencies."

Her smile instantly vanished. The last thing she wanted was Evan Blake slipping into her thoughts uninvited. She'd help him win the contest, then she'd never have to see him again. Problem solved. Or, at least, *part* of the problem.

Pulling up the conversation thread with her aunt, she quickly composed her second text—another snip of the unwanted tether inexplicably drawing her toward a man she barely knew.

Can you arrange a date with Varun for sometime next week?

She waited a few seconds, her heart pounding harder than it should as she stared at the screen. A date—a specific day and time—that's all she needed to banish Evan from her thoughts. Something concrete. A commitment to a man like Varun, her perfect match in every way.

After waiting another minute without a response, she stuffed her phone in the back pocket of her linen trousers, determined to switch her focus to where it belonged—on Abby and the Serena situation.

From the moment Serena arrived, the woman had been impossible to please, as if she'd already made up her mind about Abby's inn, and simply wanted to get the ordeal over with as soon as possible.

Nadia had met influencers like Serena before. Jaded. Self-centered. Callous. They'd lost their passion for discovering beauty and excellence and sharing it with the world. They'd lost their joy and purpose. And instead of doing their job with kindness and respect, recognizing the heavy weight of responsibility on their shoulders, they walked through life with cold indifference to the hopes and dreams they trampled along the way.

But Abby wouldn't go down without a fight. And neither would she. They'd show Serena what made Blessings on State Street, and Blessings Bay, so magical. And if any place would aid their efforts, it was CeCe's.

Nadia pushed through the front door, welcomed by the enticing aroma of freshly ground coffee and the sweet, buttery scent of pastries rising in the oven.

The café owner, CeCe Dupree, had successfully combined her love of coffee, crafts, and specialty cakes into one cozy and eclectic space. The result was a whimsical and unique atmosphere where customers could take a craft class and learn a new hobby like needlepoint or calligraphy while they enjoyed gourmet beverages and baked goods.

Today's pairing featured something called a Bicerin, accompanied by a butterscotch biscotti, and a beaded suncatcher strung with colorful sea glass. If Serena wasn't impressed, Nadia would seriously question the woman's ability to find pleasure in anything.

"Nadia, over here!" Abby waved from a table by the window where she sat with Serena. The two women already had drinks, dessert, and their bead kits spread out on the table.

"Sorry I'm late." Nadia settled into the vacant seat.

"We're just getting started," Abby assured her. "Sage saw you come in and went to grab your drink."

Nadia leaned over Abby's steaming cup, inhaling a heady whiff of dark chocolate. "What exactly is a Bicerin?" she asked, pronouncing the word like *bicep*.

"It's actually pronounced bee-cherr-een," Serena corrected, smiling for the first time since they met. "It's Italian. And it's delicious. Like a mocha, only a million times better."

"Serena's been telling me all about it." Abby raised her eyebrows in a silent you-won't-believe-her-good-mood expression. "She met the inventor of the original drink, Al Bicerin, in Turin, Italy. She was there reviewing the Casa Della Francesca, a boutique bed-and-breakfast converted from an old palace. Isn't that incredible?"

"It sounds amazing." Nadia noticed the way Serena's entire face brightened as Abby recounted her story, as if she'd been transported back to a happier time and place. As if, once upon a time, she actually enjoyed being the Savvy Sojourner.

"It was," Serena said dreamily, mentally twirling on the hilltops of Turin à la Julie Andrews. "The experience was truly transformative. The process to make the drink is surprisingly complicated. It has three layers. Coffee, cocoa, and frothed milk. Each ingredient must be a precise temperature and expertly layered or the whole thing won't work. They've been trying to replicate it in the States for years, but most people get it wrong. Due to a translation error from Italian into English, a lot of coffee shops use cream instead of frothed milk. And at that point, it's no longer a true Bicerin."

"So." Nadia dropped her gaze to the transparent mug on the table, noting the three distinct layers. "What do you think of this one?"

Serena lifted the glass to her lips and took a slow, languid sip, surprising Nadia with another smile. "*Perfetto*," she said in flawless Italian, setting the glass back down. "Almost as good as the real thing."

Nadia refrained from tossing Abby a triumphant high-five. Finally, the Ice Queen had melted. All thanks to a hot cup of coffee. Abby beamed at her from across the table.

"I can't wait to try it," Nadia said, genuinely curious.

As if on cue, Sage Harper flitted toward them. The bevvy of beaded gold bangles stacked on her arms jingled as she set the glass on the table.

"Hi, Nadia! It's so lovely to see you again." Sage flashed a sunny smile—the kind of smile that could make the most shy, anxious introvert relax.

"You, too. When I saw that today's class involved beadwork, I hoped you'd be teaching it." Sage made the most incredible artwork out of sea glass, and she'd designed a stunning tree topper for Abby last Christmas featuring Donnie's military dog tag. Too bad her art didn't pay the bills. Last time they spoke, she'd mentioned her discouraging job hunt. "Are you working here full-time?"

"No, I'm still trying to figure out what I want to be when I grow up." Her lighthearted laugh didn't quite mask her deeply buried discontent. At twenty-seven, Sage was only a few years younger, but as far as Nadia could tell, she'd yet to find her life's passion. "I was just telling Abby how much I admire her for opening Blessings on State Street. It takes guts to go after your dream. Even though it's obvious she's a natural-born innkeeper."

A snort escaped Serena, and she hid it poorly behind a sip of coffee.

Although Serena had the decency to look embarrassed by her blunder, Nadia wanted to nudge the metallic toe of her sandal into the woman's shin. How could she be so rude and insensitive? "I couldn't agree more," she said a little more emphatically than necessary.

Abby blushed and stared intently at her half-eaten biscotti as if the flecks of butterscotch spelled a hidden message.

Fury burned in the pit of Nadia's stomach. Had there been a few hiccups during Serena's stay so far? Sure. But Serena had arrived early. And she didn't care what the woman said, something felt off about the supposed mix-up. Abby wouldn't have messed up a detail that monumental. And she'd been trying her hardest to make up for it ever since. As far as Nadia could tell, Serena wasn't giving Abby a fair chance. And she was determined to find out why.

Her phone buzzed in her pocket.

Sage had tactfully changed the subject and moved on to

the suncatcher instructions, so Nadia surreptitiously slipped out her cell, expecting a follow-up text from Ishani.

Logan? He only had her number for emergencies.

Can you occupy Serena for a few hours after your class? I have a surprise for Abby.

Chapter Thirteen

EVAN

"I don't know what's wrong with me, Dad. I can't stop thinking about her." Evan paced by his father's bedside, his steps keeping time with the rhythmic beeping of the heart monitor. "There's just something about her. She's like a mystery waiting to be solved. On the outside, she's this strong, self-assured woman. She's not afraid to say what she thinks. And people listen. I may not always like what she has to say, but I respect her honesty."

He paused, realizing his opinion of Nadia had swiveled a complete one-eighty in less than twenty-four hours. In his grief, he'd interpreted her review as overly critical. He hadn't been able to see the kindness laced in her words—the way she'd tried to spur him to succeed.

Last night, after she'd confronted him on the beach, he'd dug out a copy of her review—the one he'd stuffed in the bottom drawer of his desk as a hidden token of his failure. All the same words that had wounded him a year ago still jumped off the page, but this time, he noticed the other words, too.

. . .

Tammy's Taffy is clearly dedicated to quality and craftsmanship. If you're looking for a classic, quintessential saltwater taffy, you can't go wrong with any of the four standard flavors. However, if you're searching for something extraordinary, something to delight and excite your taste buds with its whimsy and unexpected undertones, this brand isn't for you. While the current offerings lack nuance and originality, I'm hopeful the company will challenge their confectionary creativity and offer their customers a sensory-dazzling experience worthy of their skillset.

If he'd had the emotional bandwidth to see beyond her criticism, he would've seen she was one hundred percent right.

"Beneath her blunt, say-it-like-it-is exterior, there's a surprising softness. A kindness." Evan turned to face his father, who lay still, eyes closed, lost in a state of perpetual sleep. "She's special, Dad. I can feel it. And part of me wants to see if we could have something—to see if she'd even be interested. And the other part wants to run."

He waited in the silence, aching for his father to respond while knowing he wouldn't. In his thirty-one years of life, he'd never been this open with anyone. He'd never poured out his heart, unloading every convoluted, incoherent thought that sprang to mind. And especially not with his dad.

The closest thing they'd ever had to a heart-to-heart was the day of his mother's funeral. He'd found his father on the back porch, sitting in a rocking chair that didn't sway, staring at the moonlight scattered across the ocean. He'd sat next to him on the stuffed ottoman his mom had used to prop her feet, leaving her rocking chair glaringly vacant.

Behind them in the kitchen, casseroles, soups, and pies his father would never eat littered the countertops. They'd sat for several minutes, neither saying a word as the waves lapped against the beach below.

Evan still remembered watching a ship in the distance as it floated across the dark surface until it disappeared from sight as he told his father, "I'm moving back home. I'm going to take over Mom's business."

His father didn't respond at first, his own gaze fixed on the black, murky expanse where the water merged with the invisible horizon line. Finally, his dad rested a hand on his shoulder and said, "She'd like that."

From that moment on, they never spoke of it again. He never told his dad what the decision had cost him. It simply became the new norm.

Why he'd decided to spill his guts now, he wasn't sure. Maybe the silence felt safe. Or maybe he thought his father should know the truth—that his son still needed him.

"Knock, knock." Mia poked her head in the doorway. "Mom sent these over." She rattled a box of salted caramel pralines. "She says your mom used to bribe your dad with them whenever she wanted the gutters cleaned, so it might work in this scenario, too." She smiled, but it slipped away the second she saw his father lying in the hospital bed.

Evan's heart twisted at the glint of panic in her eyes. It mirrored his own fears whenever he let his mind dwell on the seriousness of the situation.

"He's been like this for three days?" she whispered.

"Four." Evan watched the range of emotion on her face shift from shock to sadness to resilient optimism.

"Hey, Big Mike." She paired the nickname she'd used as a child with a fresh, cheerful smile. "I just finished working on Jayce Hunt's latest romantic comedy. There's this super cheesy scene where they kiss in the rain, and I had to cook seven pounds of bacon to get the rain sounds just right. You would've loved it."

While she regaled his dad with more Foley artist anecdotes, Evan sat down for the first time that morning. His shoulders slumped as some of the tension slid to the floor. He and Bonnie had been trading off time at the hospital during the day, but he'd been spending every night on the foldout cot. He wanted to be there the second his dad regained consciousness.

I'll just close my eyes for a second....

He woke to someone prodding him in the ribs.

"Hey, Sleeping Beauty, go home and get some rest," Mia chided from her perch on the chair beside him. "I can hang out here for a few more hours."

"No, I'm fine." He rubbed his eyes and sat up straighter. "What'd I miss?"

"I was just telling your dad about your big crush. Or have you already told him?" She smirked.

"Crush? Are we back in junior high?" he deflected, not about to admit that yes, he had already told his dad about Nadia.

"We might as well be," she teased. "You were too chicken to ask girls out then, too."

"Okay, let's say I did have a *crush*," he said, emphasizing her ridiculous word choice. "What would be the point in asking her out? She lives in LA."

"LA's not the moon, Ev. You don't even need a passport." As soon as the playful rebuttal left her mouth, she grimaced. "I'm so sorry. I forgot that Hillary—"

"Don't worry about it," he interrupted before she could say another word about his ex. "To be honest, I don't think I could even focus on dating someone right now." His gaze drifted to his dad, and Mia's followed.

She squeezed his hand. "He's going to come out of this. I know he is." Evan nodded, his heart numb. "In the meantime," she said gently, tightening her grip, "you gotta start living your life. *Your* life, Ev. Not anyone else's."

She pressed a kiss to his cheek, as if the sweet gesture would soften the sting of her words. He knew she cared about him, so why did it feel like he'd just been punched in the stomach?

Chapter Fourteen

LOGAN

LOGAN TUGGED on the edge of the checkered blanket, ignoring the nervous energy sloshing around in his stomach.

Abby would be back from CeCe's any second, and the impromptu picnic needed to be foolproof. Which was saying something, since he'd been Fool Numero Uno for months. He couldn't believe it had taken him this long to figure out his next move.

The sound of clinking bottles drew his attention to the wicker basket. Bing sniffed and rooted around inside like a potbelly pig on the prowl.

"Hey, man. That's not for you." Logan flicked his hand at the pup to shoo him away, but Bing merely lobbed him a lazy glance before shoving his face back inside the basket. A moment later, he resurfaced with one of the warm garlic rolls between his teeth.

"You can have *one*. But that's it. This picnic is my big chance to get things back on track with Abby. Got it?"

Bing plopped onto the blanket to enjoy his treat, stretching his legs behind him as if he didn't have a care in the world. In the process, he knocked over the small vase of pink peonies Logan had picked from the garden.

Logan lunged for it, setting it upright before all the water drained and soaked the blanket. "Haven't you ever heard three's a crowd?" he mumbled, wondering what Bing was doing outside on his own. "Does Verna know you're gallivanting through the neighborhood?" He glanced over his shoulder, across the street. The frilly, floral curtains in the front window fluttered closed, but not before he glimpsed Verna's telltale orange hair. "Aha. Why am I not surprised? You're on a covert operation, aren't you? She sent you over here to spy on me. Do I need to pat you down for a wire?"

Bing gazed at him with big, innocent eyes, and Logan chuckled. "I thought we were pals. I'll remember this betrayal the next time you want belly scratches." He tried to sound stern, although they both recognized the empty threat. Besides, everyone in town knew Verna was allergic to minding her own business. If he'd wanted guaranteed privacy, he would've arranged the picnic in the backyard. But his surprise hinged on Abby spotting him the moment she got home.

"I hope your reconnaissance report will reflect my efforts. I think Verna would be proud. I've followed all her unsolicited advice about paying attention to the details. I ironed the blanket, grabbed the fancy dishes, and picked up takeout from Abby's favorite restaurant. And the flowers are a nice touch, don't you think?" He'd decided to nix the candles due to their recent rendezvous with the fire department. "Am I missing anything?"

Finished with his roll, Bing batted a prickly pine cone,

then pulled back his paw, shooting Logan a look of annoyance.

"Hey, don't get snippy with me. That's not for you. It's for Abby." He grabbed the pine cone and readjusted the emerald-green ribbon tied at the top while Bing watched, clearly not impressed. "I know it's goofy, but I don't make the rules. When you like a girl, you'll do dumb stuff, too."

He'd rolled his eyes the first time he heard about the Timber Ball tradition. Apparently, asking a girl to the dance by giving her a pine cone tied with a ribbon—and not just *any* ribbon; it had to be green—didn't seem as strange to the rest of the town. He recalled hearing something about a pine cone being a vessel for the seeds, and the seed represented a seed of love, which grows into a tree, blah, blah, blah. He didn't normally buy into the sappy schmaltz and kooky customs, but for Abby, he'd fill the entire bay with pine cones, green ribbons and all.

Bing had moved on to the white gift box tied with a pale-blue bow.

"Hey, watch where you're putting those grubby paws." Logan swiped the box, moving it out of Bing's reach. "This is a gift for Abby."

Bing raised his thick, wrinkly eyebrows, as if to imply he hoped it was better than a pine cone.

"While it's none of your business, I think she'll like it." When he spotted the decorative frame in the gift shop, he'd immediately been drawn to the smooth, hand-carved drift-wood. And he knew exactly which photo he wanted to place inside—a snapshot Sage had taken of him, Abby, and Max while they were searching for sea glass along the secluded beach by their home a few weeks ago.

The first time Sage had shown it to him, he'd merely stared, too shocked to speak. It was as if she'd crawled inside his mind and stolen one of his dreams—a favorite, frequently recurring dream where he, Abby, and Max were a happy, uncomplicated family, without caseworkers, constant check-ins, and a jam-packed calendar.

In this sepia-toned fantasy, full of sunsets and serene family strolls, he no longer had muscle spasms, and Max didn't have nightmares about his father's shipwreck. And Abby... Well, Abby had never looked more blissful and beautiful.

The moment Sage had snapped the photo, he'd been teasing Abby about how tiny her footprints looked in the wet sand—like a little leprechaun. She'd swatted his arm, and he'd retaliated by splashing her with water from the tide lapping at their feet.

Abby had laughed, the kind of head-thrown-back, hair-flowing-in-the-wind, face-upturned-toward-the-setting-sun kind of laugh that filled his dreams.

The smile on Abby's face in Sage's snapshot resembled the same smile he'd admired in Donnie's photo all those years ago, the one his friend had kept above his bunk during basic training. He remembered envying Donnie for finding a woman like Abby. A woman who was not only beautiful but radiated warmth and kindness. A woman with a smile that could light up the world.

He never imagined that one day that smile would be for him.

"Logan?" Abby's voice tugged him back to the present day.

He tucked the box behind the picnic basket before scrambling to his feet, his pulse hammering.

This was it. Time to take his shot.

Abby stood on the street, her gaze sweeping the unexpected scene.

He knew he should say something, to explain. But his brain couldn't focus on stringing words together. It was too busy drawing a mental picture and committing it to memory.

Abby was the embodiment of perfection in her faded blue jeans and striped cotton T-shirt. Her dark, glossy hair hung in loose waves that grazed her shoulders, and his fingers curled at his sides, yearning to thread through the soft strands that always smelled like lilacs and whatever she'd baked most recently.

He wasn't a stranger to the dull ache of wanting something he couldn't have, but this time, the intensity took him by surprise. If one of them didn't speak soon, he wasn't sure what he'd do, but it would probably involve vaulting across the lawn for a kiss he could already taste.

"What's all this?" she asked, breaking the heavy silence. "Nadia said you needed to speak to me about something. I worried the leaky faucet might be worse than we thought."

"No, I fixed that. It's such a nice day, I thought we could have a picnic lunch." Why did he suddenly sound like an awkward teenager fumbling over an invitation to prom? *Get it together, man.*

"A picnic?" Abby inched closer, as if the entire scene could be an illusion.

"Yeah, well. We don't get many opportunities to spend time together, so I thought I'd make one."

"And Bing decided to join us?" Abby smiled at their third wheel, who'd snuck another garlic roll when Logan wasn't looking.

The pudgy-pawed little thief. Logan tossed him a scowl that said, *I thought we had a deal.* "I'm pretty sure his collar is bugged so Verna can eavesdrop on our date."

"This is a date?" Abby asked in a soft, hedging voice, as if she assumed she'd misheard.

Smooth. Real smooth.

He leveled Bing with a look that said, *See what you did,* then sighed. He needed to get back on track. Facing Abby, he shoved aside all pride and pretense, finally ready to bear it all. "I hope it's a date. A long-overdue one." He took a step toward her. "Abby, I've been an idiot. Life has been so hectic with the inn, Max, and my..." He paused. *My what?* Injuries? Insecurities? He settled on a vague description. "Stuff."

Taking another step, he closed the gap between them. He stood so close, he could trace the amber halo around her hazel eyes, and as she held his gaze, so open and unwavering, his throat went dry. It took all his strength to keep talking when his lips tingled to taste hers. "I've been sitting on the sidelines, waiting for the right time, for things to settle down. But I realized that if I keep waiting for perfect, time'll run out."

Need and adrenaline blazed through him like jet fuel ready to combust. *Focus.* With nowhere else to go, he leaned forward, a fraction of an inch, and lowered his voice to fit the intimate space. "I'll be honest." His words somehow sounded both soft and rough, revealing how badly he wanted her—wanted *this*, the two of them, together. "I don't know how this is supposed to work. But I do know you're the most incredible woman I've ever met. That I'll *ever* meet. And I'll do whatever it takes to make this last. That is, if you're willing to give me another chance," he added, realizing with gut-wrenching awareness that he could be too late. He let one agonizing second pass before prompting, "What do you think?"

"I think..." she said slowly, her voice a breathy blur. "I think it's about time." Without another word, she clutched the front of his shirt and rocked onto her tiptoes.

He took her mouth with his, sinking into the feel of her soft lips, the gentle pressure that grew exponentially with each passing nanosecond, the surge of desire that barreled against him with the blood-draining power of pulling 9 Gs. He felt lightheaded, shaken to his core, and more alive than ever.

And he relished every second.

A throat cleared.

Blast. With a low, guttural groan, Logan broke away from the best kiss of his life and focused his bleary gaze on the source of the unwanted interruption.

Carla Delgado, Max's social worker, flashed an apologetic grimace. "I hate to interrupt, but I have some big news. About Max."

Chapter Fifteen

ABBY

ABBY BARELY NOTICED the scalding liquid dripping from her hands or the fractured remnants of delicate porcelain scattered on the sitting room floor.

Carla's words slammed against her again and again, like a hammer tied to a spring. *We've located one of Max's relatives. And she wants custody.*

Dazed, Abby blinked, struggling to reorientate with her surroundings.

They'd invited Carla inside for a cup of tea, to share her news in a more private setting. Apprehension whirled in Abby's stomach, and she'd mentally tallied the possibilities, but this? She hadn't been prepared for this.

"I'm so sorry! Are you all right?" Carla's concern pulled Abby back to the present, rescuing her with the impulse to focus on someone else.

"I'm fine." Her vision focused, and she realized Logan had gathered the broken teapot in a pile and had pressed a towel over the damp patch in the carpet. She met his gaze and recognized the same thinly veiled distress she felt roiling inside. She wiped her wet hands on her jeans. "You caught me by surprise."

"I understand." Carla offered a kind smile. "Frankly, we were all surprised. We've been looking for Max's family members for so long, I think we'd all given up hope."

"What happened?" Logan sat on the edge of the couch, gently tugging Abby beside him. "Why now? Max's been in foster care for months."

Abby gripped his hand tightly, grateful for the strength and security of his grasp.

"I know. And she feels terrible about that. She's Max's great-aunt on his father's side. She was living abroad in France and hadn't heard the news until she tried to get ahold of Max's dad. Apparently, he sent her a card with an update on Max every year around this time. When she didn't receive the card, she tried to call. And when she couldn't get through on his cell phone after several attempts, she did a little digging and discovered what happened."

"She lives in France?" Abby's chest tightened. *They couldn't relocate Max overseas, could they? What about school? Soccer? All his friends? What about* us, a silent voice screamed.

"Temporarily. She's a traveling nurse. But her contract with her current hospital just ended, so she recently moved back to the States."

"I see." Abby kneaded her bottom lip, trying to wrap her head around the barrage of details. The woman was a nurse. That was good, wasn't it? She could take care of Max. And she was probably kind and caring. That was important.

Despite her best efforts to be positive, she couldn't quiet

the voice inside her heart asking, *But will she love him as much as I do?*

"I realize this is difficult." Carla's warm brown eyes softened with all the kindness and compassion Abby had come to appreciate. "You two have done a wonderful job caring for Max. But we've found it's often in the child's best interest to be with family if at all possible."

Abby involuntarily winced. She wanted to shout, *But we are his family.* But what good would that do? She knew what Carla meant. They weren't blood. And when it came to the blood, sweat, and tears of raising a child, blood always won.

"I'll try to make the transition as smooth as possible," Carla continued. "I'd like Denise to come by tomorrow after school to meet Max. Does that work for you?"

Denise. Denise Smith. Abby turned the woman's name over in her mind, trying to smooth the rough edges, but nothing helped. The woman was a stranger. And she planned to take Max away. "Will Max remember her?"

"Probably not. She said the last time she saw him, he was too young to form any lasting memories. But Max's father kept her updated. Here." Carla leaned forward in the armchair and handed her a photograph. "He sent her this in his most-recent letter. It looks like it was taken in Blessings Bay. Probably shortly before he was lost at sea."

Abby studied the snapshot, tears welling, blurring the border. Max stood on the promenade, the bay in the background. He was smiling, but it wasn't his usual smile. It lacked the brightness in his eyes, as if he didn't quite feel like smiling. Strange that out of all the photos his father could've sent, he chose this one.

"So, this is really happening?" Abby's throat cinched around her words, and Logan squeezed her hand.

"Saying goodbye is always hard," Carla said softly, "but you two made a difference in Max's life. Remember that."

Abby nodded, fighting tears as she handed back the photograph.

Carla stood. "This will be hard on Max, too. He'll need your help to adjust."

Abby read between the lines. *Stay strong. Be positive. Don't break down.*

"We'll do whatever we can to make this easier for Max." Logan slid his arm around her shoulders, and the second Carla let herself out, Abby collapsed into him, letting the tears fall.

In one moment—one conversation—her world had crumbled. The pain seared through her, as real and deep as the day Donnie died. And yet, the whispers of her fears and insecurities rose above her quiet sobs, shaming her for her tears. How could she mourn the loss of a son who was never really hers?

Buried in grief, she cried until she had nothing left to give. When she finally lifted her swollen, tear-streaked face, she met Logan's gaze. It was like looking through a window wet with rain, and through the glassy surface, she saw heart-wrenching sadness. He'd miss Max, too. But he was trying to be strong. For her. For Max. For all of them.

"What are we going to do?" she whispered.

"The only thing we can do," he said in a voice raw and raspy with emotion. "We have to tell Max."

Chapter Sixteen

NADIA

WHILE SERENA CHATTED about her stay in a Swedish ice hotel, Nadia stole a quick glance at her phone on the dash mount. A blank screen stared back at her.

Still no text from her aunt. Or Abby. She was hoping for an update on Logan's surprise. Instead, the mystery only deepened. About an hour after his first text, he'd sent another, asking her to stall Serena until after dinner. What did he have planned that spanned most of the day? Her heart skipped a few beats. Could it be a proposal?

An involuntary smile stretched across her face as she navigated the winding road skirting the staggering cliffside. The sun sank into the ocean, splashing pinks and yellows across the glistening water like melting sorbet. Abby and Logan could be on the beach right now, Logan down on one knee, framed by the soft, romantic glow of the sunset. Was it too soon? Maybe. But not everyone needed years of dating to know they'd found The One. Most likely, she and Varun would only have a handful of dates before tying the knot.

The thought left her oddly unsettled, and she pushed it from her mind.

"Is that the restaurant?" Serena gasped from the passenger seat.

"Yep. It's called The Sawmill." She followed Serena's gaze straight ahead. A large rustic building illuminated by twinkling lights stood at the edge of a headland, high above the sea. White-tipped waves splashed against the steep cliff face, flinging salty spray into the air like welcoming fanfare.

From a distance, the old sawmill resembled a provincial barn with wide, rough-hewn beams, worn and weather-beaten from years of exposure to the sun and sea air. But as they parked on the mainland and followed the lantern-lit pathway, the elegant details of the reconstruction came into view. Inky black wrought iron curved and twisted into a striking archway draped in more glittering lights. And as they approached the entrance, an amber glow shone through the stunning stained-glass insets of the double doors, inviting them inside.

Awe and delight sprawled across Serena's face as the hostess led them through the main room of the restaurant onto an expansive deck that jutted out over the sunset-soaked water. Candles and kerosene lamps flickered on the tables, and Nadia had never seen Serena look happier than when they were seated by the railing with an unobstructed view. Maybe she'd finally won over Little Miss Faultfinder.

Nadia silently thanked Sage, who'd pulled strings as a part-time server to snag them a last-minute reservation. Abby would be pleased to hear Serena had enjoyed perusing the shops on Main Street that afternoon and appeared even more dazzled by their dining experience.

"I have to admit," Serena said, as if reading her thoughts, "I'm impressed. In fact, this entire day took me by surprise."

"I'm glad. I had a great time, too." Nadia returned Serena's rare but refreshing smile. Away from the inn, Serena had transformed into a completely different person. She was curious, adventurous, and excited to learn new things. She hadn't made one snarky comment when Archie, the local grocer, gave them an impromptu and long-winded lesson in Blessings Bay's rich logging history. In fact, she'd sounded genuinely interested. This Serena—the Savvy Sojourner who relished exploring new locales—Nadia actually liked. If only this version would stick around long enough to write Abby's review.

At a nearby table, a woman gasped in delight and shouted an emphatic, "Yes!"

Nadia turned, expecting to find a man on one knee, diamond engagement ring in hand. Instead, the woman cradled a spiky pine cone as if she held a priceless gem.

"That's odd." Serena eyed the couple with confusion.

Nadia smiled. "Abby told me about this. Apparently, it's how men in this town invite their dates to the Timber Ball."

"The what?"

"The Timber Ball. It's some big fancy dance at the end of the festival. If you'd arrived when Abby originally intended, you'd have gotten to attend."

"Excuse me?"

Shoot. You've put your foot in it now, Nadia.

Tension sizzled across the table, so thick and pervasive, panic settled in Nadia's chest. Once again, her big mouth had shoved her headfirst into trouble. Sure, she had her suspicions that Serena had arrived early on purpose. But she couldn't figure out *why*. What motive could the woman possibly have for moving her reservation? Did she think the spontaneity made her reviews more authentic? Regardless, she wouldn't get her answer tonight. And she didn't want to make this worse for Abby. Time to backpedal. *Fast*.

"I just meant it's a shame you won't get to experience one of the town's main events." She softened her tone, hoping to smooth things over. Her efforts were met with a cold glare. *Try again. Build some rapport.* "Do you like your job? I love being a professional product reviewer, but sometimes, the sense of responsibility can weigh on you."

"You're a professional reviewer?" Serena's interest outweighed her irritation. *Okay, now we're getting somewhere.*

"Full-time for the past six years. It started as a hobby. I simply shared my favorite products on social media, and it snowballed from there. Eventually, companies sought me out for endorsements and collabs. And before long, I formed a paid review service."

"Really?" Serena's entire posture instantly changed. Leaning forward with both arms on the table, she asked, "So, companies pay for your opinion?"

"And for the exposure. I publish all my reviews on my website and across all my social media platforms. If I like a product, it's basically a public endorsement. And they can quote my review in their own advertising."

"How much does that cost?"

"My fees vary based on the type of product."

"Sure. But how much extra for a good review?"

"What do you mean?"

Serena sighed, as if she found Nadia's confusion tiresome. "How much do you charge companies for the Nadia Chopra seal of approval?"

"Oh." Nadia balked at the implication. "I don't charge anything for that. I never guarantee a positive review."

Serena frowned and slumped back in her chair, clearly deflated.

Was Serena a sellout? And if so, what was she doing in Blessings Bay? There was zero chance Abby had paid for a positive review. If anything, Serena seemed bound and determined to give Abby a *bad* one.

Nothing made sense. And if she had to "play nice" and refrain from being confrontational for Abby's sake, Nadia had no idea how she'd solve the mystery.

At the very least, she hoped Abby's night had turned out better than hers.

Chapter Seventeen

ABBY

ABBY GENTLY CLOSED the door to Max's room, and the fragile fissures of her heart broke even further. How many more times would she get to tuck him in at night? How many more times would she stroke his hair as he fell asleep and place a feather-soft kiss on his forehead? How many more times would she get to say *I love you*?

Numb with grief, she stood in the dark, shadowed hallway, unable to move as her heart drifted away from her body, searching for a place to hide.

"Are you okay?" Logan's voice, low and raspy, coated with equal parts sadness and concern, wrapped around her like a tether, anchoring her to something safe and steady.

"No," she whispered back, the searing sting of hot tears burning her eyes, branding her memory with Max's crestfallen face. He'd tried to be brave. He'd tried to understand. But she could see the fear in his eyes. Fear of the unknown. Fear of leaving the safety of their home. And fear that if he left, his father wouldn't be able to find him.

His last concern—the one that had turned his beautiful

brown eyes red and watery—had broken her heart the most. He still needed so much healing. He needed someone to walk beside him through the grieving process, someone who understood that kind of loss. Someone like her and Logan. But what could she do? She had no legal standing to say or do anything.

Logan pulled her against him, and she inhaled his comforting scent—crisp and fresh like the ocean air after an unrelenting rain. He ran his fingers up and down her back in long, soothing strokes, smoothing the tattered edges of her heart.

When her breathing finally slowed to a more stable rhythm, he murmured, "Put on something warm and meet me out back."

She dressed in a daze, vacillating between feeling too much and nothing at all. With her thick cardigan wound tightly around her, she stepped through the French doors into the stillness of the night. As if they could sense her troubles, the cold air caressed her cheeks, and the ocean waves welcomed her with their reassuring rumble.

Her gaze panned the vast, starlit sky, widening in surprise when she caught sight of the secluded stone patio. Gold-and-amber flames flickered in a round brick fire pit, lending light and warmth along with several tealight candles nestled in dainty glass jars. Two mugs sat on the rim of the fire pit, steam curling in delicate wisps.

Logan waited for her on the wicker love seat, and when he spotted her walking toward him, he lifted the edge of the large wool blanket.

She slid beneath the soft fabric, relishing the warmth and comfort of his body so close to hers. For the past few months, she'd daydreamed about elaborate dates and extravagant meals followed by romantic moonlit strolls along the shore. But isn't this what she *really* wanted? Someone by her side for all life's highs and heartaches. A partner. A man with modest, simple means who made her feel like the most special person in the world.

Her heart thudded a resounding *yes* as Logan handed her a mug of hot chocolate and their fingers grazed, eliciting a burst of electricity. Her heart had healed after Donnie. Maybe, just maybe, it could survive this, too.

She snuggled closer, grateful when he wrapped his arm around her shoulders. For several minutes, neither spoke, companions in their silence, savoring the subtle crackle and pop of the smoldering logs. In the stillness, her thoughts swirled and tumbled, eventually making their way past her lips.

"It's ironic," she said softly, watching the flames flutter and dance, scattering sparks into the obsidian sky.

"What is?" His fingers curled around her upper arm, strong and affirming.

She gathered a breath, surer than ever that he could be trusted with her innermost thoughts. "When Max first came to live with us, I was terrified. I had no idea what I was doing. I mean, I'd always wanted to be a mom. More than anything. But I thought I'd start with a baby and learn as I went along. But with Max, it felt like being thrown into the deep end. What do I know about raising an eight-year-old boy? I was so afraid I'd mess up and get everything wrong. But now..." Her voice broke, and Logan drew her closer. "I don't want to say goodbye." The words escaped in a strangled whisper, scraping against her raw throat.

"I know," Logan murmured, resting his head against hers. "Neither do I."

He held her for another long moment, then reached for a flat, rectangular gift box she hadn't noticed before. His eyes shone with a hesitant glint as he placed it in her hands.

"What's this?"

"Open it."

She tugged on the ribbon, unraveling the bow until the soft satin puddled in her lap. Her pulse thrummed as she lifted the lid. What could it be?

With one last glance at Logan—who radiated a palpable blend of nervous energy and hopeful anticipation—she pulled back the thin layer of tissue paper. Her breath caught.

There, nestled in pale-blue paper, an image of pure joy glowed in the firelight. Tears sprang anew. She remembered that day so clearly, as if her heart had captured the same photograph. She'd never felt so at peace—so complete.

A tear trailed down her cheek, slid past her chin, and dappled the smooth glass of the photo frame.

"Shoot. I'm sorry, Abs." Logan raked his fingers through his hair, his muscles tense with self-reproof. "I knew I should've waited to give it to you. I just thought after what you said to Max tonight—about how no matter where he was or where he lived, he'd be in your heart forever—well, I thought maybe you'd want the photo after all. I feel like a jerk."

He reached for the frame, but she cradled it against her chest. "I love it. It's perfect. Thank you."

Another tear fell, and Logan gently gathered it on his fingertip. His touch sent a ripple of warmth across her skin.

"I wish there was something I could do," he said in a low, gravelly breath.

"Just be here."

He gripped her hand, his gaze peering so deeply into hers, she was sure he could read each unspoken thought. "I'm not going anywhere."

With his words, the world fell away. The stars dimmed, the ocean stilled, and the flames flickered out.

Every muscle in her body drew toward him with magnetic force, and she longed to lose herself in his kiss.

But before their lips could meet, a creaking door overhead snapped the world back into focus.

Nadia was home. And she'd opened the door to her balcony.

Abby closed her eyes, determined to block out the world, to hold on to the moment, if only for a few more seconds.

The scraping of metal chair legs made her shudder, like nails on a chalkboard, weakening her resolve. Nadia must have repositioned one of the bistro chairs with plans to enjoy the moonlit view before bed.

With a shaky sigh, Abby opened her eyes.

"I should tell Nadia what happened and find out how things went with Serena." Even as she said the words, she wished she hadn't.

"Yeah, sure." He straightened, but the shift in posture did little to mask his disappointment.

She stood. Slowly. Regretfully. "Thank you. For this." She hugged the frame to her heart.

He smiled, but his eyes looked gray and muddied.

Her gaze dropped one last time to their blissful faces forever encased in glass—a perfect memory trapped in time, never to be repeated. The sobering thought struck her with as much force as a physical blow.

Max had been their linchpin. Living together, doing life together, had been for Max, to give him a stable home.

With Max gone, what else would change?

NADIA

STEAM MISTED Nadia's face as she stirred, but she barely noticed. Her thoughts swirled like the creamy masala chai in the copper pot, always coming back to the same upsetting truth—Max was leaving.

Abby had slipped into her room late last night, her eyes red, swollen, and dry, as if she'd already cried her allotment of tears. As she spoke, her words dropped like verbal grenades, decimating the beautiful future Nadia had envisioned for her friend. Her heart ached for Abby's loss. And Logan's. And hers.

She'd never been like Abby. She'd never felt the same gut-level longing for motherhood. Maybe someday. But definitely not before she'd mastered the elusive art of maintaining a lasting relationship. And yet, she'd quickly come to adore Max and loved him like a nephew. She couldn't imagine their lives without him. And she was hard-pressed to believe this newfound great-aunt could be a better mother to Max than Abby.

To make matters worse, on top of this huge loss, Abby

had to focus on Serena, Queen of Complaints. Maybe even the Savvy Sellout. She didn't have the heart to tell Abby about their dinner conversation last night, in case it added to her already astronomical stress level.

Fortunately, Serena would be gone all day on an ecotour led by Zander Barnes, owner of the nursery and nature preserve, Hilltop Haven. While Serena rode the Timber Train, admiring the redwoods, then waded through knee-high ferns, learning to identify the local flora and fauna, Abby would get a much-needed break. That is, before Denise Smith arrived.

Nadia shuddered and swept aside a strand of hair dampened by the steam.

"Is it supposed to boil over like that?" Evan's voice broke through her thoughts, drawing her attention to the frothy plume threatening to spill down the sides.

"Shoot." She quickly lifted the pot off the burner. The milky foam settled—along with her racing pulse—and she placed it back on the stove.

"Can't leave you alone for five minutes," he teased, heaving a bag of raw sugar onto the counter.

He'd stepped out to sign for a supply delivery, leaving her in charge of the chai. She'd made it so many times, she could do it blindfolded. But apparently, not brokenhearted.

"It's fine. We'll let it come to a boil one more time, then lower the heat and let it simmer."

"I can't get over how good it smells." He leaned over her to inhale the heady scent of cardamom, black pepper, cinnamon, cloves, and ginger.

She tried not to notice the rough stubble on his jawline or the way his hair smelled faintly of mint and coconut.

When he finally stepped back, she released the breath she'd been holding. "It's almost done."

She pulled a small jar from the package her mother had overnighted and unscrewed the lid.

"What's that?" Evan eyed the yellowish-amber-colored spice with unveiled curiosity as she dropped a pinch into the stone mortar.

She smiled, appreciating his inquisitiveness. From the moment she arrived that morning—and they'd decided to make a pot of chai before working on the taffy recipe—Evan had wanted to know every last detail. In contrast, in all the years they'd dated, Brian would happily drink a cup of chai whenever she made it, but he never once cared about the process. He never cared about the history or tradition or what it meant to her family. Turns out, he never really cared about her, either.

Pushing the melancholy thought aside, she said, "It's mace, the sister spice to nutmeg. Technically, they're from the same tropical plant. Nutmeg is the seed, and mace is the waxy webbing that protects the seed. When it's dried, it's called a blade." The pungent, earthy aroma punched the air as she ground the pestle into the dry skin.

"What's it taste like?"

"It's hard to describe. But I guess you could say it has warm, sweet flavor notes and a subtle pop of pine. It's a little peppery, too." She sprinkled the fragrant powder into the pot and closed her eyes, letting the spicy sweetness wrap around her like a comforting hug. For a brief moment, she allowed herself to be transported somewhere else, somewhere safe, free from the day's worries. When she finally opened her eyes, she found Evan watching her. "What?" She straightened, suddenly self-conscious.

"This drink is special to you." His words were soft, almost tender, and sent a strange tickle down the back of her throat.

"It's been a part of my life for as long as I can remember. It's reassuring. No matter what I'm going through, I can always count on it for a sense of calm." Her cheeks flushed. Why had she been so open, so honest? The words had simply spilled out. She rushed to add, "I realize it's just tea and that probably sounds ridiculous."

"Not at all. I get it. That's how I feel about surfing."

"Surfing? You're kidding."

"I never kid about surfing." His lips twitched in an irresistible half smile that made her stomach spin.

She flicked off the burner. The entire room suddenly felt uncomfortably hot. "I can understand how surfing might be exhilarating, exciting, even freeing. But calming? Definitely not. The ocean is a deathtrap."

"A deathtrap?" His sea-green eyes flickered with amusement.

"You think I'm overreacting, but let's talk facts. The ocean is chock-full of deadly hazards. Sharks, rip currents, undertows, poisonous jellyfish." She ticked them off on her fingers. "And did you know there are black holes? Yeah, that's right. Black holes. They're not just in outer space, my friend."

"Black holes?" He chuckled as if he didn't believe her.

"I'm serious! They're these enormous vortexes that suck you into oblivion. Some are so large, they're even bigger than the greater Los Angeles area."

He continued to gaze at her with the half-cocked grin that rankled her nerves and made her skin sizzle. In desperate need for some liquid calm, she added a generous pour of maple syrup to the pot—her mother's variation in lieu of cane sugar—then divided the steaming beverage equally between two glasses. "Feel free to fact-check me." She slid the second glass toward him before wrapping both hands around her own, willing its cathartic magic to cure her hammering heartbeat.

"I believe you. But I'm not convinced oceanic black holes are a common occurrence. I've been surfing since I could walk, and I've yet to be sucked into a mysterious vortex."

"Well, don't say I didn't warn you. The ocean is far too unpredictable to be safe."

"Do you only do things that are safe?" The teasing tone vanished, and something in his gaze—an intense, intimate level of interest—made her shiver.

For a fleeting moment, she wanted to throw caution aside and dip her toes in the deep end. But the last time she took a risk, she'd nearly drowned.

Whatever you do, stay on dry land.

As if privy to her thoughts, he stepped closer. "Come surfing with me."

"What?" She took an involuntary step back.

"I'll show you that it's not as scary as you think. It's only fair."

"Fair?" She swallowed the hard lump in her throat, but it didn't budge.

He bridged the gap, backing her against the counter. "You introduced me to your source of calm, so I get to show you mine."

He wore an easy smile while every fiber in her being fought off a five-alarm blaze. "Technically," she said slowly, scrambling for an escape route, "you haven't tried mine yet."

Still smiling, he reached for his glass.

She watched, her gaze glued to his lips, her heart thrumming a beat she'd never heard before.

Why did it suddenly feel like her whole world hinged on this one sip?

Chapter Nineteen

EVAN

EVAN MARVELED at the mouthwatering blend of sugar and spice as the masala chai slid down his throat. In a strange way, the alluring combination reminded him of Nadia—strong and provocative yet surprisingly sweet.

"Okay, you were right. This beats any chai tea I've ever had. It's like night and day."

Her entire face brightened at his compliment. "I always love hearing I'm right," she teased. "And if we can figure out how to get the same flavor notes in a batch of taffy, I'm confident you'll have a shot at winning the competition."

They spent the next three hours testing recipes, trying to match the flavor without sacrificing the creamy texture. Normally, he would've been frustrated by each failed attempt. But in this case, he didn't mind. Each tweak in the recipe meant more time with Nadia.

"This is the one. I can feel it." Nadia's dark eyes glowed with optimism, and Evan couldn't tear his gaze away. She looked beautiful, disheveled, and unbelievably beguiling. Her smooth skin glistened from the steam, and silky strands of her ink-black hair had slipped from her ponytail, framing her face. A huge smudge of spice—maybe cinnamon or clove—streaked her right cheek, and it took all his self-control not to brush it away. But he knew once he touched her, he wouldn't want to stop at smudge removal.

"Ready to give it a try?" He tore off a piece of taffy, wavering between two conflicting desires: to finally achieve a winning recipe and to never let this moment end.

"Let's try it at the same time." She pinched off another piece and held it aloft, a few inches from his face.

Hmm... So, she wanted to feed each other? He'd be up for that.

She counted down from three, and they simultaneously popped the taffy into each other's mouths. He'd tried to be discreet, but accidentally—or more likely, *instinctively*—grazed her perfect pillowy lips in the process. Just a tad. But enough that his limbs instantly turned to Jell-O.

"Oh, wow," Nadia moaned, and Evan tried to focus on the flavor notes melting across his tongue. Warm spices and cool cream melded into a magical amalgamation that surpassed anything he'd ever imagined. He could eat buckets of this stuff.

"You're a miracle worker," he mumbled as he reached for another piece.

"As much as I appreciate the praise, we did this together. But I agree, it's pretty incredible."

"That's an understatement." He savored another bite, still amazed by the complexity of flavors. "I gotta admit. I was skeptical at first. But this has blue ribbon written all over it. We make a good team." As soon as the words left his mouth, he cringed. Could he be any more of a romantic-comedy cliché?

"In the *kitchen*," she added with unabashed emphasis, as if she needed to drive home her point.

Why did he suddenly feel the need to convince her they'd be good together in other areas, too? Resisting the urge to argue, he poked his head through the swinging door that led to the main shop. "Hey, Bonnie. Do you have a sec? I'd like you to try something."

He stood beside Nadia, ignoring the strange and unexpected impulse to hold her hand while they waited for Bonnie's reaction.

"Oh, my." Bonnie's blue eyes widened with delight. "You two really outdid yourselves. It's delicious. In fact, I may need to rethink my entry if I want to compete with this." Her features softened as she met Evan's gaze. "Your mother would be so proud, honey."

An uncomfortable tightness seized his throat, and he barely managed to squeeze out a small and inadequate "Thanks." But he knew Bonnie could read beyond his words.

"What are you calling it?" she asked.

"I don't know." He hadn't thought that far ahead. "Chai Tea Taffy? What do you think?" He turned to Nadia.

"While I appreciate the alliteration, *chai* actually means *tea* in Hindi, so you'd be naming it Tea Tea Taffy, which might be a little redundant. Plus, it's technically *masala* chai. Although the terms are interchangeable in some regions of India, chai is traditionally black tea with milk, while masala chai includes the addition of spices like cinnamon, cardamom—"

"And mace," Evan interjected. "Which I learned about

for the first time today." There were few things he found more fascinating than watching Nadia make her mother's recipe. He wanted to learn everything there was to know about her and her family's traditions.

"That's right." Nadia smiled. "You get a gold star."

He grinned, loving her playful side. "How about we call it Masala Chai Taffy?"

"I like it. It's simple and says what it is. And with your branding, it would be Tammy's Masala Chai Taffy, so you'd get a little of the alliteration, too."

Warmth wiggled around Evan's heart at the mention of his mother, and he added another tally to Nadia's Nice column. Although it would be far easier to be indifferent, he couldn't help being drawn to her. And it only intensified the more time they spent together. Not for the first time, he wished he could ask his dad for advice. The thought left a gaping hole in the pit of his stomach. One he couldn't fill with taffy, no matter how much he ate.

"You two should go out and celebrate all your hard work," Bonnie suggested, helping herself to another piece.

"We've definitely earned it, but I can't today." Evan hoped he didn't sound as disappointed as he felt. "I promised Mia she could take me shopping for a new suit this afternoon. She said, and I quote, 'If you wear board shorts to the Timber Ball, I'll email everyone I know a copy of your Madonna photo.'"

"Your what?" Nadia asked, and Evan instantly regretted sharing the details of Mia's threat.

Bonnie laughed. "When they were kids, they went through this phase of listening to all my old records. For some reason, Mia talked Evan into dressing up as Madonna and—"

"It was a dare," he interjected in his defense, as if it made a difference.

"That's right. You two were always talking each other into doing silly things. Like the time Mia had to wear a wet suit to school for a week." Bonnie shook her head in amusement. "Anyway, she put together his outfit and did his makeup, then snapped a Polaroid, which she must've kept all these years."

"As blackmail," he grumbled.

"I'd pay a lot of money to see that," Nadia teased.

"Not as much as I'd pay Mia *not* to show you. Hence the coerced shopping excursion."

"Didn't Mia tell you?" The high-pitched twinge in Bonnie's tone set off his meddling-mother-meter. "I asked her to cover the shop for a few hours so I can sit with your dad at the hospital. She won't be able to go shopping after all." He sensed a *but* coming, so he didn't celebrate just yet. "But," she added on cue, "she thought maybe Nadia could go with you." She turned her far-too-innocent smile on her unsuspecting target. "Since you clearly have impeccable taste."

"Oh." Caught off guard, Nadia glanced between them.

He rushed to her rescue. "I'm sure she has better things to do than help me pick out a new suit."

"Do you, dear?" Bonnie asked, barely refraining from batting her eyelashes.

"Well…" Nadia hesitated. "Abby and Logan have something important going on later today, so I'd planned to hang out in town until this evening. I, uh, brought a book with me."

Bonnie flashed a triumphant grin, and Evan realized she'd just sealed their fate. "While I'm a book lover myself, I'm sure you can put it off for one more day. After all, you wouldn't want Evan to wind up with some tragic powder-blue suit with sequins, would you? The boy is clearly helpless when it comes to fashion." She tossed a pointed stare at his cargo shorts and cotton tee with a surfboard graphic and the words *Sorry, I Was in a Board Meeting* printed on the front.

"Hey, I'm standing right here."

"I know, dear. But you can't pair a tie with a punny T-shirt and call it evening wear. So," she said, turning back to Nadia, "do you think you can help?"

"You make it sound like I'm a menace to society," he mumbled under his breath. While he wasn't opposed to spending the afternoon with Nadia, he wasn't thrilled with Bonnie's strategy.

"Bad fashion affects us all," Bonnie said gravely.

Nadia's lips twitched, and Evan sensed she fought hard to contain a snicker of amusement. *Great.* How was a guy supposed to recover from this level of embarrassment?

"I'll do my best, but I can't make any promises." Nadia met his gaze with good-natured laughter in her eyes, thankfully taking it all in stride.

"Your best is all we can ask, dear. You kids have fun." Bonnie popped another chunk of taffy in her mouth and tossed him a not-so-subtle wink before sauntering out of the kitchen.

He'd have a thing or two to say to the mother-daughter co-conspirators later, but for now, he had to figure out how to salvage his dignity. "You know you don't have to do this, right?"

"I don't know. Saving society from your ill-advised fashion choices seems like a pretty serious responsibility. I don't want to let Bonnie—nay, the *world*—down." This time, she let her laughter bubble to the surface, and he had to admit, he liked the sound. Even if it was at his expense.

"Okay, Chuckles. I'll be your Ken doll for the day if you come surfing with me when we get back."

The laughter fizzled out. "Even if I wanted to accept your proposal, I couldn't. I didn't pack a bathing suit."

"Then it looks like I won't be the only one buying a suit today."

He grinned. The day had just become a lot more interesting.

Chapter Twenty

LOGAN

LOGAN HAD EXPERIENCED this kind of silence before. It was the kind of deafening silence that signaled danger. The kind of silence that amplified every heartbeat. Every breath.

He fixed his gaze on Abby and Max, seated on the couch to his right. They wore the same apprehensive expression, although Abby tried to mask hers with a forced smile. Carla and Denise sat across from them in matching armchairs, casually sipping tea as if their sitting room wasn't a battlefield over Max's future.

"So, Max," Denise said a little too sweetly, as if she'd chugged a gallon of maple syrup. Why did some adults feel the need to sound like cartoon characters whenever they talked to kids? "Carla tells me you had a pizza party after soccer practice today."

Max stared blankly, and Logan didn't blame him. She hadn't exactly asked him a question. After a long pause, Max offered a simple "Yeah."

"Do you want to tell Denise what position you play?"

Carla prompted, in her best soft-spoken, family-facilitator voice.

"Defense." He swung his legs, back and forth, back and forth, occasionally scraping the carpet with his heels. *Swish, swish, swish.* A dead giveaway of his simmering nerves.

Logan's jaw clenched, and the veins in his neck throbbed. He'd dealt with his fair share of crummy situations—situations he couldn't control. He'd come to terms with his accident, a fiancée who'd ditched him during his darkest hour, and muscle spasms that seized his body at the worst possible moments. But when it came to someone he loved—someone like Max—he couldn't stomach the helplessness.

"Wow. That's an important position." Denise laid it on thick, overinflating her words like a helium balloon ready to burst any second. "You must be very good."

Max's brown eyes brightened at her compliment, and Logan had to hand it to the woman. She had a knack for flattery. In the twenty minutes since she'd arrived, she'd praised the decor, Abby's desserts, and even lauded his landscaping skills. Although she seemed nice enough, she was overselling herself. In fact, everything about her was too much. Her hair was too blond, her teeth too white, and her clothes too flashy. Like a facade, built to impress. Maybe even deceive. He couldn't put his finger on it, but something about her felt off.

"How's school?" she continued in her irritating I'm-talking-to-a-toddler tone. "Do you have a favorite subject?"

"I like geography. We made a map of the oceans today."

Denise's gaze darted to Max's backpack, propped on the floor by his feet. "May I see it?"

"Sure." Max shrugged, then hoisted the backpack onto his lap.

Denise scooted forward and set the teacup on the coffee table, her sharp green eyes glinting like a hawk, poised on its prey.

Logan met Abby's gaze over the top of Max's head, and in one glance, he could tell she'd noticed the same thing: Denise seemed oddly eager all of a sudden. Who got that excited over third-grade cartography?

Max rummaged through his backpack, removed a folded sheet of paper, then zipped the main compartment closed.

Denise shifted back in her seat, her countenance slightly less interested as Max unfolded the map on the coffee table and showed them his sketch of the Pacific Ocean.

"This is Blessings Bay." He jabbed a crescent-shaped squiggle colored in with blue pencil. "And these are the Tanti Islands. My teacher says *tanti* means a lot or very many or something like that. She says it's because there are a lot of islands. Like, a bunch. And some are really small. Like, smaller than a soccer field. I didn't know islands could be that small. But I think my dad might be on this one." He pointed to a green blob with a big red X drawn over it, like X marks the spot. "It's called Stargazer Island because there aren't very many trees, and you can see the whole sky from everywhere. My dad likes looking at the stars. So, I think if his boat sank and he had to swim to shore and build a shelter for a while, he'd pick this one."

Logan's heart slammed against his chest like a wrecking ball of unwanted emotion. After all this time, Max still hadn't given up hope. Any day now, his father would come back for him. Max never wavered, never doubted. Logan had faith like that once, when he was a child. Even after his grand-parents told him about the car accident, he sat by the window every day after school for two weeks straight, waiting for his parents to pick him up. When he finally realized they weren't coming, something shifted inside. He stopped believing in a lot of things that day.

"Max," Carla said gently. "Remember what we talked about?"

Max stared at the map, tracing the cluster of islands with his finger. "That my dad lives in Heaven with my mom now."

The hollowness in his little voice was like a gut punch. Logan met Abby's gaze again, and the tears in her eyes hammered another blow. Abby and Max were hurting, and there wasn't a single thing he could do about it. He wound his hand into a tight fist and dug it into the couch cushion.

"It's very complicated," Carla continued, carefully navigating the tricky terrain. "But they've been looking for your dad for a long time, so it's very likely he won't be coming back. Which is why it's important to place you in a more permanent home with—"

"But I want to stay with Abby and Logan!" With an unexpected burst of emotion, Max sprang off the floor and scrambled back onto the couch, sandwiching himself between them.

Logan instinctively wrapped his arm around Max's shoulders, every innate urge intent on protecting him. He saw Abby grip Max's hand, keeping her tears at bay with a willpower that amazed him. She must be crumbling inside, and yet, she held it together for Max's sake.

"I know you've been very happy here, Max." For the first time, Carla's soothing, steady tone faltered. Was she having second thoughts? She gathered a stabilizing breath, and sat up straighter, like a soldier bound by duty. "Unfortunately, the courts must consider several factors, and they think it's best if you live with Denise. She's your father's aunt, which makes her your great-aunt. Although you were very young the last time you saw her, and you may not remember, she's family. And in time, you'll get to know each other and form a bond, just like you did with Abby and Logan."

Max's small frame still leaned into him, as if he wanted to disappear into the throw pillows. Logan hugged him tighter, and bit back a retort about bureaucracy and broken systems, knowing it would only make things worse.

Abby, in all her calm, maternal wisdom, swiveled on the couch to face Max. Taking both of his hands in hers, she looked into Max's eyes with a depth of motherly love that made Logan's own eyes tingle.

"We're not going anywhere," Abby assured him without an ounce of hesitation. "We're family, and we want to stay in your life. We'll come visit you, and talk on the phone, and you can come back and stay with us for a few days, too. We already talked to Denise about it, and we all agreed. Isn't that right?" Abby asked Denise.

"Yes, absolutely." Denise nodded, smiling her too-sweet smile at Max.

"What about Ron?" Max asked, slowly relaxing after Abby's reassurance.

"That's his rabbit," Logan explained, wondering how she'd react to the news of an unexpected pet.

"He can come, too!" Denise responded a little too quickly, as if she'd say anything Max wanted to hear.

Logan was tempted to add *And what about his pet*

python? to see if he could get a reaction out of her. Something about the interaction rubbed him the wrong way, but he couldn't explain it. She'd been too easygoing, too unflappable. Assuming custody of an eight-year-old boy would change her entire life, but she didn't seem to grasp the magnitude of the situation.

They chatted for a few more minutes, and set up another time for Denise to come over, then Logan walked the two ladies to the door while Abby stayed in the sitting room with Max.

"Mind if we talk alone for a sec?" Logan asked Denise after Carla said her goodbyes and headed for her car.

"Not at all." She let her keys dangle in one hand while she waited for him to speak.

Logan cleared his throat. "I wanted to make sure you knew Max's story. He's been through a lot. His last foster parents essentially used him as slave labor, making him cook and clean while they pocketed all the money from the state. Money that was supposed to go toward raising Max. On top of that, they operated a stolen credit card and identity theft ring, and when the cops got close, they bolted, abandoning Max without a second thought." Anger burned in his chest just thinking about it. "Add all that to the fact that his mom died when he was a baby and he recently lost his dad, and the kid's had a pretty rough go of it."

He paused, expecting Denise to respond to what he'd shared, but she merely stared, her expression unreadable. Her keys jangled as she shifted her feet.

"Anyway, I thought you should know," he said, regaining his bearings. "He's a good kid, and it's about time the adults in his life start looking out for him. We all want the best for him, right?" He emphasized his question, indicating with his tone that her response would qualify as a binding agreement.

"Of course," she assured him with the sort of warm, friendly smile meant to assuage his concerns. "You don't have a single thing to worry about."

Nothing in her gaze or tone of voice gave him reason to doubt. So, why couldn't he squelch the strange churning sensation in the pit of his stomach?

Chapter Twenty-One

NADIA

NADIA ABSENTMINDEDLY SCROLLED through her phone, mentally suppressing the swarm of butterflies frolicking inside her stomach since early that morning. With each flap and flutter of their obnoxious little wings, they repeated the same infuriating message: *You like Evan Blake. And whether you admit it or not, this is the most fun you've had in a long time.*

Drat. Why did they have to be right?

After they'd cleaned up the kitchen at Sweet Blessings, Evan took her to Steam Engine Sammies, a quirky sandwich shop operating out of an old steam train engine. They'd sat at a cozy bistro table shaded by fragrant redwoods, serenaded by the sounds of the sea in the distance.

Nadia smiled at the memory. She'd plucked all the pickles off her turkey on marbled rye, and Evan had snatched them off her plate. When they were dating, Brian had pestered her for disliking something so universally popular, as if he considered her aversion to the fermented cucumber a moral failing. When she'd told Evan not to waste his breath—he'd never convert her over to Team Pickle—he'd cocked his head and asked, "And why would I want to do that? If you don't like pickles, there's more for me." She couldn't explain it, but something about his statement stuck with her.

"I feel like I should be humble-bragging about my Maserati with my country club cronies," Evan called over the dressing room curtain, visible from the neck up. Sticking his nose in the air, he added in a snobbish accent, "It takes a glacial 2.9 seconds to go from 0 to 60, my good man. And the interior? Leather and Zegna silk. Ghastly."

Nadia laughed. "Joke all you want, but it's a classic suit that should be a staple in every man's closet."

"And what if I don't have a closet?"

"You must have a closet."

"I used to." Evan reached for the suit jacket and slid it off the wooden hanger. "You know the row of bungalows by the beach?"

"The ones that look like a Crayola box?"

"Yeah," he chuckled. "I live in the seafoam-green one."

"It's next to the adorable dark-blue bungalow with white shutters?" She'd noticed it had a for-sale sign.

"Yep. That's the one. It's a studio and only had one closet."

"Had?"

"I took the door off and converted it into Sylvester's room."

"Sylvester?"

"My roommate."

"Your roommate lives in a closet?"

"It's more spacious than you'd think." He shrugged on the jacket. "Sylvester is a red rock crab I found one day while

I was surfing. Both of his claws had been crushed, and he wouldn't have survived out there on his own."

Nadia's heart melted at the thought of Evan rescuing a wounded crab. And when he stepped from behind the curtain—his toned, athletic frame draped in the most gorgeous smoky-gray wool—her heartbeat stopped altogether. She stared, slack-jawed like a simpering schoolgirl.

"Well, Fairy Godmother," Evan teased. "Am I ready for the ball?"

Nadia lifted her jaw off the floor and regained her composure. "You still need a tie, but other than that, it's perfect."

"Sorry, no can do."

She raised an eyebrow.

"I don't wear ties," he clarified. "Never have, never will."

"Surely, you're exaggerating." She couldn't fathom a grown man refusing to wear a tie.

"Nope."

"What about on your wedding day? You'll wear a tie then, won't you?"

His features clouded for a brief flash before he ducked behind the curtain again. "I don't plan on it. And if I pick the right woman, I don't think she'll mind."

Nadia decided to avoid that land mine. "What's your aversion to ties?"

"You mean besides the fact that I like breathing?"

She rolled her eyes. "They're not that bad."

"Okay, maybe not. But I still don't like having something tied around my neck." He squirmed out of the jacket. "And I don't see the point. Clothes should be comfortable."

Nadia glanced at her chic wedge sandals. The tight straps

pinched her skin, and the gold buckles dug into her ankles, but they looked fabulous. "I think every fashion designer in the world might disagree with you. But I'll give you a free pass on the tie." She eyed his surfer-style flip-flops in the gap below the curtain. "What about shoes? Do you find closed-toe footwear morally reprehensible as well?"

"Only the ones with tassels." He grinned, and she found herself smiling back.

"Well, we can agree on that, at least. So, you have dress shoes?"

"They might be a few decades behind the current trends in Hoity-Toity Magazine, but I think they'll pass your inspection."

"You make me sound like a drill sergeant." She averted her gaze as he unbuttoned his shirt, even though she couldn't see below his neck. But despite her best efforts, she couldn't help envisioning his well-defined physique. He must have a six pack, at least.

"Nah." He grinned over the curtain, and she caught a glimpse of his muscular shoulders. *Settle down, stupid butterflies.* "If there was a fashion branch of the military, you'd be a five-star general, for sure."

She laughed at the absurd mental picture. "That may be the strangest compliment I've ever received."

"Have you always been into nice clothes?"

His question propelled a deeply buried memory to the forefront of her mind. She was nine and had begged her mother to wear her favorite dupatta to school. She'd adored the royal-blue silk, intricate embroidery, and glittering beads. The moment she'd wrapped the long, shawl-like scarf around her shoulders, she'd felt like a princess. She didn't even mind that the large swath of fabric engulfed her small frame and trailed along the ground. But when one of the other girls had mocked her for wearing a "fancy tablecloth" to class, she'd cried in the bathroom stall, determined to dress more "normal."

With a sharp shake of her head, she dismissed the thought, grounding herself in the present. "Not always. But I learned pretty early in life that clothes are the quickest way to make a first impression. We project who we want the world to see with what we choose to wear."

He stepped out of the dressing room in his cargo shorts and T-shirt. "And who do you see when you look at me?" The husky catch in his tone made her think his question was more than casual curiosity.

In other circumstances, she would've been able to answer quickly, without a moment's hesitation. But with Evan, it was more complicated. She'd seen the kind heart behind the clothes. And she liked what she saw.

"I see someone who appreciates the simple things, who finds worth in the people around him, not in the material. But I also see someone struggling with his identity, who's torn between his own dreams and obligation." Her final thought spilled out of her before she had time to soften the blunt edges, and she could tell from his hardened expression that she'd struck a nerve.

His gaze bored into hers, intense and unwavering. "And what do you want people to see when they look at you?"

She opened her mouth to respond, but the words caught in her throat. A few months ago, she would have given her answer instantly. But now? She honestly wasn't sure anymore.

Chapter Twenty-Two

NADIA

NADIA CAST a surreptitious glance at Evan as she slipped off her cotton shift dress. His gaze remained fixed on the task of waxing his surfboard. *Darn.*

She knew exactly what image she wanted to portray when she picked the black monokini swimsuit earlier that afternoon. The high neckline and full backside coverage said *modest* and *classy*. But the narrow side cutouts that accentuated her cinched waist said *subtle yet flirtatious*.

Naturally on the curvier side, she worked hard on her figure. While the diet gurus would have to pry carbs out of her cold, dead hands, she stuck to a disciplined exercise routine to offset the calories. She may never have visible abs or slim hips, but she'd managed to ward off a tummy pooch while still eating all the freshly baked naan her heart desired. And for some reason, she hoped Evan had noticed.

She neatly folded her dress and set it next to her wedge sandals and cross-body purse on Evan's front porch steps. He'd said to make herself at home when they'd arrived at his place to change into their swimwear, but she'd found that impossible. Evan's beachy bungalow fit the term *bachelor pad* to a T. Although clean and relatively tidy, it begged for a decorator. From the worn flea-market furniture to the stack of outdated surfing magazines on the scuffed coffee table to the mismatched dishware, she guessed he'd been single a long time. Her mind reeled with questions about his dating history, but she couldn't devise a casual way to ask.

She reached for the wet suit draped over the railing—the one he happened to have on hand close to her size. Maybe the wet suit could be her excuse to probe about his love life? Or lack thereof.

But before she could pose a single question, he handed her a small glass jar. "You'll want to put this on first."

"What is it?" She hid a smile when she caught him steal a glance at her legs. So, he *had* noticed.

"Anti-chafing balm."

She wrinkled her nose. "Ugh. Is it necessary?" Anti-chafing balms were notoriously sticky.

"Only if you want to avoid an annoying rash from the wetsuit."

With a heavy sigh, she unscrewed the lid and dabbed a minuscule amount onto her arm. "Wow. This is really silky. And it smells heavenly. Where did you get it?" She examined the nondescript jar, inhaling the pleasant scent of minty coconut. "It doesn't have a label."

"That's because it's homemade."

"By who?" She slathered on more balm, keen to buy a few jars for herself. If it worked, she'd write a raving review, too. When he didn't respond, she met his gaze. Her eyes widened as realization dawned. "Wait. Don't tell me *you* made it?"

"Why do you sound so surprised?"

"I don't know. Maybe because not many men make DIY beauty products."

"It's medicinal. And I didn't like any balms on the market, so I did a little research, whipped up a few batches, and ultimately landed on this formula."

"What makes it so silky?" With one foot propped on the arm of an Adirondack chair, she massaged the buttery balm onto her leg, working from her ankle up to her thigh. She caught him ogling again, and for some reason, his admiring gaze sent warm tingles over her skin, like the heat from the sun.

He cleared his throat and diverted his attention back to the surfboard. "Sorry, but that's proprietary information."

"Have you thought about selling it?" She wriggled into the wet suit, squirming a little extra to slide it over her hips.

"For half a second. But I didn't think Tammy's Taffy and Anti-Chafing Balm made sense from a branding perspective."

He had a point, but still, she was intrigued. Revolutionary products didn't come along every day. And if it actually prevented rashes, it could be a real moneymaker.

"Ready?" he asked.

"No." She grimaced, glancing warily at the ominous ocean. The blue-gray water beckoned, glittering in the late afternoon glow, as if to assuage her concerns. Aiding the ocean's efforts, the cloudless spring sky blanketed the bay with an aura of calm. Maybe it wouldn't be so bad after all?

"You're in good hands. I promise." He stepped behind her and swept aside her hair, lightly grazing her neck. She shivered, longing to feel more of his touch as his fingertips moved to grasp the zipper she hadn't been able to pull all the way closed.

"You don't want your hair to get snagged." He spoke low and soft, his breath tickling her ear.

Her toes curled into the warm sand. He stood so close she could almost hear his heartbeat above the rumble of waves. For a brief moment, she imagined what it would feel like if he slipped his arm around her waist, turned her around to face him, and—

Her fantasy abruptly ended with the loud *zip* of the wet suit.

She tried to concentrate as he explained proper positioning and pressure pads, or what he called the "control buttons" on the board, safety tips, and how to stabilize and stall the board, if needed. Each time he placed his hands on her to demonstrate a particular move, her body liquified, becoming as weak and wobbly as a jellyfish. She forgot all about their impending foray into the deadly waters.

That is, until they stood toe to tide, boards in hand.

"The water's freezing." She inched backward.

"It'll get warmer when your blood starts pumping."

She refrained from mentioning how her blood had already started pumping the instant she felt his touch. "It'll also be warmer in late August. Why don't we try again then?"

"If it means I'll get to see you again in August, I might consider it."

She glanced over in surprise, expecting to see a playful glint in his eyes. But she saw something deeper instead—something real. She'd been teasing, stalling for more time. But Evan was dead serious. And the realization scared her more than the ocean.

Rattled by the unexpected connection sizzling between them, she strode deeper into the bone-chilling water. "Then again, it's probably better to get it over with, like ripping off a Band-Aid."

"I don't advise you do that unless you want to attract all the sharks." He'd tried to sound lighthearted, but Nadia caught the note of regret. "Remember," he continued. "We're not standing on the board this time. Today is all about playing with the waves, getting a feel for things—a small taste. Standing can come later."

"Got it, coach." She sucked in a breath as the icy water crept up her legs, settling around her waist. If the sharks didn't get her, she'd freeze to death.

"Let's start here," Evan called from a few feet away, motioning for her to face the shoreline. "We'll wait for a nice clean wall of white water. No funny angles. Then we'll get in the position I showed you on the beach. Paddle four or five times before the wave hits, then about three more as you catch the wave. Got it?"

She nodded, teeth chattering as she glanced over her shoulder. A potent blend of excitement and terror rose in her throat, burning like bile. Was she really doing this? Before today, she wouldn't step foot in the ocean for all the designer heels in the world. What had changed her mind?

She instantly knew the answer. Something about Evan propelled her out of her comfort zone and made her wonder what she'd been missing. Somehow, he made it all seem less terrifying. And worth the risk.

An involuntary gasp escaped her lungs as the wall of white-tipped waves hit her back, lurching her forward. She gripped the board, muscles clenched as she rocketed toward the shore. The wind whipped her hair, and salty ocean spray stung her cheeks, but a fire rose from deep inside, fighting to get out.

Possessed by an intense urge—a *need*—she couldn't explain, she pressed her palms into the board, springing to her feet.

"Nadia, don't—"

She didn't hear the rest of Evan's warning. Before she'd fully tasted freedom, her board tipped, dumping her sideways into the waves. She couldn't have been in more than four feet of water, and yet, she couldn't find the surface. Salt burned her nose, and she fought the urge to scream, flailing her arms and legs, struggling to gain her bearings.

Was she being pulled out to sea? *Please, no!* Fear filled every fiber of her being, weighing her down like an anchor and solidifying one hopeless thought.

She never should've left the shore.

Chapter Twenty-Three

ABBY

ABBY SUCKED IN A DEEP BREATH, struggling to steady her erratic pulse as she fought an onslaught of emotions. She was drowning. Drowning in grief. Drowning in uncertainty. Drowning in her own helplessness. Everything she held most dear—from Max to the inn to Logan—was slipping through her fingertips. And she felt powerless to hold on, no matter how tightly she clung.

She sipped her Lavender Saffron Latte, oblivious to the sweet and spicy flavor notes as she tried to organize her chaotic thoughts. She'd left Logan and Max at home to finish Ron's hutch and had hoped a walk in the pleasant evening air would clear her head. When that didn't work, she popped into CeCe's for a jolting dose of caffeine but stumbled upon an unsettling sight instead.

"How long has *that* been going on?" On break, Sage plopped onto the chair beside her, her tight honey-blond curls bouncing around her shoulders. She nodded toward a cozy table for two in the back corner as she slurped her filled-to-the-brim iced tea.

"I have no idea," Abby admitted, frowning at the unlikely couple. "Not long. She's only been in town a few days."

All sunshine and smiles, Serena Scott canoodled with Zander Barnes over a plate of powdery beignets. Abby found it almost eerie to see the woman so happy, especially given her cantankerous track record.

"How do they know each other?" Sage asked, helping herself to a corner of Abby's butter pecan brownie.

"They met briefly the other day. And she went on his nature tour this afternoon. But I had no idea *this* would happen." Abby's frown deepened. She liked Zander. He was shy and sweet, while Serena made the prickliest cactus look soft and cuddly. She had a hard time imagining their unexpected romance would end in anything but disaster.

"Well, maybe it's a good thing," Sage offered. "People in love are happier and more apt to view situations in a positive light. Which bodes well for your impending review, right?"

"I suppose so." Although desperate for Serena's stamp of approval—which seemed more elusive every day—she didn't want to sacrifice Zander's heart for her own gain. "But I'm beginning to think it's a lost cause. She seems determined to dislike me."

"I can't imagine anyone not liking you. But even if that's true, it's only one person's opinion. She can't wield that much power, can she?"

Abby sipped her latte, weighing her response. Serena may only be one person, but she influenced thousands. *Millions*, even. Yes, the inn could technically recover from one bad review. But it would be hard. Serena had the reputation for making and breaking careers. And Abby had made things worse by ensuring Serena's review would be the very first. Unless the Savvy Sojourner deemed Blessings Bay a worthwhile destination, no one would give her fledgling inn a chance. "You're probably right." She forced a smile. "I'm sure it'll be fine. Besides, I've been so focused on things with Max, I've barely had time to think about it."

Sage instantly sobered. "When does he leave?"

"In three days. Carla said he could stay for the festival, but that's it." Her voice caught, and she bit her lower lip, willing the tears away.

"I'm so sorry. We're all going to miss him."

Abby nodded, too emotional to speak. How long until she could talk about Max without breaking down?

Ever the sensitive soul, Sage came to her rescue by switching topics. "How long is Serena staying?"

"She leaves the same day as Max." Abby tried not to think about how empty the house would feel.

"She's leaving before the Timber Ball?" Sage sounded surprised.

"Yes. Which, I admit, is strange. I thought I'd booked her arrival for right before the festival. You know, to put our best foot forward."

"That's smart."

"Right. Which is why it doesn't make sense that I'd schedule her to arrive so early in the week and check out right before the spring's biggest event. I can't figure out how I made such a huge mistake." She'd written down the correct dates on her calendar but must have mixed them up when she spoke to Serena over the phone. Hopefully, online reservation software would solve that problem. That is, if her inn could survive long enough to afford it.

"Don't be too hard on yourself," Sage offered kindly. "You've had a lot going on. And your inn is spectacular, with or without the Timber Ball. Anyone would be lucky to stay there."

"Thanks." Abby smiled, feeling better for the first time that day. Sage had this uncanny ability to look at the bright side, and she was grateful to count her as a close friend. If only she could keep her in her pocket for every time the world fell apart.

"And speaking of luck." Sage's green eyes sparkled. "Yours might be turning around."

Abby followed her gaze back to Serena and Zander. A pine cone with a telltale ribbon sat on the table between them. For a split second, a stab of envy pierced her heart. From the moment she'd heard about the town's quirky tradition, she'd longed for her own invitation from Logan. But with everything going on lately, a fancy ball had been the last thing on their minds.

Serena squealed, nodding like a broken bobblehead while Zander beamed in his quiet, bashful way.

"You know what this means?" Sage lowered her voice and leaned forward, brimming with excitement. "If Serena goes to the ball with Zander, she'll have to extend her stay. And unless she wants to be the biggest hypocrite, she can't book an extra night *and* give you a bad review, can she?"

Abby tried to summon a smile. Sage had a point. She should be giddy. This was good news. And yet, despite how much she had riding on Serena's review, in light of Max's impending departure, she found it difficult to be happy about anything.

Chapter Twenty-Four

NADIA

NADIA STUDIED her makeup-free face in the mirror of Evan's tiny bathroom. She'd almost drowned. She'd stepped out of her meticulously controlled world for one second and had almost drowned.

Still reeling from her wrestling match with the waves, she rubbed her upper arm. She could barely feel her biceps beneath the thick hoodie she'd borrowed from Evan, but it didn't matter. The sensation of his strong hands wrapping around her, ripping her from the water, had been burned into her memory.

He'd felt terrible about what happened, endlessly apologizing as he'd helped her inside, grabbed her some dry clothes and a towel, and explained how to work his finicky shower.

She'd insisted she was fine, and he didn't need to apologize, but deep down, she wasn't so sure. *Was* she fine? Every time she loosened the reins a little, she fell off the horse. Or in this case, the surfboard. Maybe some people weren't meant to color outside the lines?

She tilted her head to the side and gave it a good shake.

Too much salt water in the brain had her mixing her metaphors.

Gathering a deep breath, she took one last glance in the mirror. Evan's hoodie and sweatpants swallowed her whole. Her damp hair rebelled from hours beneath the straightener, curling at the ends. And with her face scrubbed clean, she hardly recognized herself.

Even after three years together, she'd never let Brian see her without makeup. Being barefaced meant she at least wore tinted moisturizer and mascara. Always the illusion of perfection.

Illusion.... Isn't that exactly what it was? A magic trick? A facade? And what had her painfully curated perfection accomplished? Nothing but devastating heartbreak and confusion. Because if Perfect Nadia wasn't good enough, what hope did Real Nadia have?

She splashed her face with cold water from the sink, hoping to reset and clear her troubled thoughts. As she patted her skin dry with the damp towel, she noticed a small jar resting on the narrow edge near the faucet. Evan's anti-chafing ointment. It really *had* worked, like a second skin.

She unscrewed the cap and dipped her finger into the silky balm, her mind whirring with ideas. What would it be like to launch a new product into the world? Challenging? Exhilarating? Rewarding? She often envied entrepreneurs the rush of taking a product to market, tackling the many facets of manufacturing and marketing. It must be so satisfying to combine creativity with streamlined planning and produc-tion procedures. Or so she assumed. Unless she had her own million-dollar idea, she'd never experience it for herself.

Nadia replaced the lid and set the jar back on the sink

where she'd found it, shoving all thoughts of Evan's missed entrepreneurial opportunity out of her mind as she slipped from the bathroom.

Evan's bungalow had an open studio-style floor plan, with a separate bathroom and the small bedroom situated in an alcove with a sliding barn door for privacy. The closet—aka Sylvester's room—fit in the space between the bathroom and alcove.

Nadia paused and peered into the spacious glass tank. Sylvester skittered over to the side, as if to greet her. "Hey, there," she whispered. "You're awfully cozy in there, aren't you?" And by cozy, she meant safe.

In truth, she needed a similar setup—enough space to live and breathe and move but with clearly defined parameters. Especially around her heart.

"Feeling better after a hot shower?" Evan's deep voice behind her made her jump. He was anything *but* safe.

"Yes, thanks." She turned slowly, wishing she'd thrown her makeup bag inside her purse that morning. But maybe it was better this way. Better for Evan to see all her imperfections. Better to squelch any interest in her, once and for all.

"I was thinking we could—" Whatever Evan was about to say fizzled in his throat. He stared, slack-jawed, sweeping his gaze from her wet hair down to his long sweatpants puddled at her feet. "You look—"

"Like I fought the ocean and lost?" she finished for him, self-conscious and frazzled as he unabashedly took in her appearance, tracing every unflattering inch of her.

"If this is how you look when you lose a fight, I don't think I could handle how you'd look if you won." His voice was thick as warm taffy, pouring over her, pinning her to the floor. Awareness flooded her body with heat, matching the fire in his eyes as he met her gaze. Against all reason and comprehension—against everything she thought she knew about society's ideals—she'd never felt more beautiful than at that moment. And she'd never felt more like herself. More *seen*.

Evan cleared his throat, dragging his attention to the cluttered kitchenette with considerable effort. "I, uh, made some of my mom's hot honey tea as a peace offering. She always used to make some when I had a bad day. I guess it was her version of masala chai."

She smiled, touched by his thoughtfulness, equal parts relieved and disappointed by the sudden shift in conversation. Had he been about to kiss her? She definitely hadn't imagined their connection. Or the desire in his eyes. And the possibility both thrilled and terrified her.

As Evan led her through the front door, two mugs of tea in hand, she cast one last glance at Sylvester, safe in his tank. He wouldn't have survived on his own in the wild. And neither would she.

They stepped into the cool evening air, and Nadia momentarily forgot her fears. The soft, pinkish sheen of the setting sun bathed the bungalow in a magical glow. Tiki torches lined the short, sandy pathway to the beach, where two Adirondack chairs sat beside a stone fire pit built in the sand. White twinkle lights wound along the porch railing and an instrumental rendition of "Can't Take My Eyes Off You" emanated from a retro-style Bluetooth speaker on the front step. The soothing sounds of the ukulele and bongo drums paired pleasantly with the hum of the ocean and gentle crackling of logs. And despite her less-than-ideal experience earlier, she suddenly saw the appeal of a quaint, unassuming beach house.

"Here ya go." Evan handed her the smooth stoneware mug once she'd settled into her seat.

"This smells delicious. What is it?" The hot tendrils of steam carried a hint of citrus, tickling her nose.

"Honey, cinnamon, and grapefruit juice."

Subtle and sweet, the flavor notes evoked a lovely calming effect the second she took her first sip. Her muscles relaxed, and she sank deeper into the smooth wooden chair, relishing the warmth of the fire. "It's so peaceful here. I can see why you never left Blessings Bay."

"Who says I never left?"

"Oh. I guess I just assumed, since you took over your mother's business."

For a moment, he didn't respond. He leaned forward, his forearms propped on his knees, hands folded. The glowing embers illuminated his sculpted features in the dimming light, and although there wasn't more than two feet between them, he looked miles away.

Chapter Twenty-Five

EVAN

EVAN STARED INTO THE FIRELIGHT, lost in his thoughts as the sky drifted from pinks and gold to dusky blues. "I moved back home a year ago. After my mom died."

He closed his eyes, blocking out the flickering flames. But he still felt their warmth. Much like that day on the beach, when he got the call that changed everything.

He'd surfed all afternoon. The waves at Venice Beach had been epic. Blissfully exhausted, he'd built a steady blaze in one of the vacant fire pits and relaxed long into the evening.

Everything had been right with the world.

Until his dad called. Crying. He'd never seen his father shed a tear. He'd never heard his voice break. Michael Blake epitomized strength. But on that day, his father had wept. And so had he.

"I'm so sorry, Evan," Nadia said softly. "I can't even imagine that kind of loss. You must miss her so much."

He clenched his hands around the mug, oblivious to the heat burning his palms. He'd done nothing but miss her for the past year. Everything he did, he did for her, to keep her memory alive. But what good had it done? He felt less like himself every day. And his father? His throat tightened and his eyes grew hot. "Some days are harder than others. But I'm glad to be home. To be near my dad."

"How is he?" Her voice, quiet and gentle, overflowed with compassion, lowering his walls.

He normally exerted great effort to avoid the topic, fatigued by all the well-meaning questions. But with Nadia, he wanted to let her in.

"The doctors don't know when he'll wake up. Or *if* he'll wake up." He'd never said those words out loud, too afraid to give voice to his greatest fear. And even now, as they hung in the air like a dark cloud, he worried he'd given them life.

"I'm so sorry." As she spoke, she tenderly touched his arm, infusing the simple platitude with a depth of raw, vulnerable sincerity that surprised him.

"Thanks," he murmured, his mouth too dry to speak above a gravelly whisper. His gaze fell to her hand, and his heart hammered inside his chest at the intensity of the connection. How could someone he'd known for such a short amount of time speak to his soul in such a profound way?

Warily, he lifted his gaze to meet hers, unsure he could handle the level of intimacy while she still had her hand on his arm. Her dark eyes gleamed in the firelight, and her thick, inky-black hair fell in glossy waves around her face. For a moment, he forgot how to breathe. How could someone be so beautiful? It didn't seem humanly possible.

His pulse thrummed, quickening with each passing second. What would she do if he kissed her?

Before he could find out, she withdrew her hand and

wound it around her mug again. He sensed an invisible divide rising between them as she asked, "Where did you live before moving back home?"

He swallowed the longing in his throat and shifted his gaze back to the fire. "LA."

"LA?" She sounded surprised.

"Yeah. Who knows? We could've run into each other in a coffee shop and never even knew it."

"Which part of LA?"

"We lived in West Hollywood."

"We?"

"Me, Mia, and my friend, Jayce. We all moved to LA after high school to pursue a life in showbiz." Even back then, he hadn't known what he'd wanted. He'd followed someone else's dream because he didn't have one of his own. After all these years, had anything changed?

A faint wisp of an idea tugged at the back of his mind— the same one that threatened to complicate his life whenever it crept into his subconscious. And just like he always did, he reminded the internal instigator that he couldn't run his own business *and* his mother's.

Suppressing the subliminal desire, he told Nadia, "Mia became a talented Foley artist and—"

"A what?"

"A Foley artist. She makes sound effects for film and TV. Rain, footsteps, cracking bones. That's all Mia."

"And your other friend?"

"He attended UCLA to become a screenwriter. But one semester, he acted in one of his own scripts for a class project, and the rest is history."

"Wait." She turned to face him, eyes widening. "Don't tell me you're friends with *the* Jayce Hunt."

"Is there more than one?"

"You mean, Mr. Hollywood Heartthrob who's been the lead in every notable romantic comedy for the past five years is from Blessings Bay?"

"Don't forget the one action movie where his character never got so much as a single scratch despite several scenes with explosions and relentless gunfire." He cracked a smile. He'd never let his friend live that one down.

Nadia shook her head in disbelief, and Evan waited for her to make a not-so-subtle comment about how she'd love to meet Jayce one day—as most women did when they learned about his connection to the superstar.

Instead, she asked, "And what about you? What's your contribution to Tinseltown?"

"Are you saying you didn't see my star on the Hollywood Walk of Fame?" he asked with mock offense.

"I must've missed it." She grinned back, and not for the first time, he marveled at how gorgeous she looked when she smiled.

"Sad to say, my rise to fame ended at prop guy. But if you need a collapsible dagger for a convincing knife fight, I'm your man."

"I'll keep that in mind," she teased. "Did you enjoy it?"

"It had its moments. But mostly it paid the bills. I never cared about that stuff the way Jayce and Mia did. Me, I lived to surf."

"Did you ever consider surfing professionally?"

"Not really. I never wanted my passion to become my

paycheck. I kinda liked surfing during my free time and getting to see Jayce, Mia, and Hillary on set."

"Hillary?"

Evan winced, realizing his mistake a fraction of a second too late. He hadn't meant to mention her name. It had just slipped out. But based on the way Nadia studied his expression, waiting for an explanation, he couldn't skirt the topic now.

"My ex. She was a makeup artist with acting aspirations."

"Was it serious?"

"Her aspirations? Yeah, I'd say so." *She crawled over my crumpled body to get to the top*, he thought morosely.

"No, I meant, were you two serious?"

He shifted in his seat. He knew what she'd meant, but he'd hoped to avoid a detailed answer. "I thought so," he finally admitted, leaning his head against the back of the chair.

"The wet suit I borrowed today... was it hers?"

"Yeah. Although, she never wore it. I'd hoped she'd go surfing with me when she came to visit, but..." He trailed off, not wanting to take the unpleasant trip down memory lane.

"What happened?"

Evan looked up at the stars, each twinkling light growing brighter as the sky darkened. "She didn't have staying power."

"What does that mean?"

"Some people only stick around when things are easy. When they get what they want. But the second things go south, they split. It's the people who stick by you through the good and the bad, no matter what happens, no matter how much changes. They're the ones with staying power. And Hillary didn't have it."

He could still smell Hillary's perfume. The strong, pungent scent of rose and blood orange still flooded his senses whenever he recalled that fateful afternoon.

His mother's memorial service had wound down, and he'd pulled Hillary aside, overwhelmed by the voice inside his head—the one he hadn't been able to quiet for the past forty-eight hours. He'd poured out his heart to Hillary, confessing his desire to stay in Blessings Bay, to continue his mother's legacy. He'd known long-distance would be hard, but he'd been committed to making it work. He'd been committed to her.

"I expected some resistance, at first," he heard himself saying out loud, realizing he'd just told Nadia the whole depressing story. "But I'd hoped she'd come around. That she'd understand why it was important to me to stay."

"But she didn't?"

"She told me I was being selfish and irrational. And that her life was in LA. How could I expect her to attend wrap parties and walk the red carpet alone?"

"Oh, Evan. I'm so sorry. That's awful."

He shrugged, trying to shake off the tightness in his chest. "At the time, I thought she had a point. I even felt bad about it. But I didn't change my mind. I stayed in Blessings Bay and called her every day for three weeks, hoping to win her back. And then—" He gathered a deep breath, grateful for the cool air filling his lungs. "Then I saw her on the red carpet. With Jayce."

"No!" Nadia bolted upright, spilling her tea. "He was

your best friend!" She wiped her hand on his sweats, seething with indignation on his behalf.

Something about the intensity of her reaction—the way she immediately jumped to his defense—made him smile.

"He still is. Jayce only took her to the premiere as a favor to me. Hillary told him I was still grieving my mom and couldn't make it, and that I wanted him to take her."

"That's downright evil." Nadia furrowed her brows in an adorable glower, and he fought the urge to kiss the frown off her face.

"Conniving, for sure. But it backfired. When Jayce found out she lied, he had her replaced with a new makeup artist."

"Good. Serves her right. There's nothing worse than breaking someone's trust."

The pointed strain in her voice caught his attention, as if she spoke from personal experience. And the sorrowful glint in her eyes cemented his suspicion.

"I take it you know the feeling?" He leaned forward, eager to reciprocate her listening ear, eager to know more about the wounds from her past—all the experiences, both good and bad, that made her who she was today.

But from the way she tensed, curving into herself like a protective shell, he wasn't sure she'd give him the chance.

Chapter Twenty-Six

ABBY

ABBY SLIPPED OUT of CeCe's without Serena noticing and mulled over Sage's remark on the walk home. Streetlamps lit her stroll, and as she moved farther away from the glow of Main Street, more stars appeared overhead.

She absentmindedly tugged her cardigan tighter, but her thoughts weren't on the chilly night air. Was Sage's assumption correct? Would Serena ask to stay another night and amend her review? And if so—and her business took off, filling the inn with an influx of guests—would the busyness dull the ache in her chest?

Somehow, she didn't think it would.

Abby pushed open the front door, and as she stepped inside, she heard music and laughter coming from the kitchen. A sharp pang shot through her. *Max's laughter*. The sweet, boyish sound filled the house. And broke her heart.

She stood in the dimly lit entryway a moment, committing it to memory.

Following the buttery scent of pan-fried bread, she found Logan and Max at the stove, flipping sandwiches on the grid-

158

dle. Logan belted out the chorus to "I Can't Help Myself" by the Four Tops while Max guffawed at his goofy dance moves. Her chest squeezed at the endearing sight. They looked so happy.

With spatula in hand, Logan lobbed the sandwich high into the air, and spun around to watch it land on the griddle, catching her eye instead.

He beamed, and she grinned back, her stomach flip-flopping at how irresistible he looked when he smiled. She expected him to stop singing once he spotted her, but he continued his lively concert performance, luring her toward him with an invisible fishing pole.

She laughed, shaking her head.

"He's reeling you in!" Max shouted in excitement, as if he'd just learned the antiquated dance move. "That means you have to dance with him."

"Oh, does it?"

Abby laughed despite herself as Max gave an emphatic nod, declaring, "It's the rules."

Getting into the spirit, she shimmied across the kitchen floor—that she'd thankfully scrubbed clean after Serena arrived—and accepted Logan's outstretched hand. He spun her a few times, crooning into the spatula like a microphone.

She loved his voice. Not because he'd win any karaoke contests. He simply sounded like home.

He pulled her into his arms, and for a moment, the music faded. She gazed into his bottomless blue eyes, breathless and brimming with awareness. No man had ever looked at her the way Logan did—intensely intimate yet unflinching. Fiercely passionate yet patient. Untamed yet incredibly tender.

Just when she didn't think she could last a second longer without tasting his kiss, an acrid aroma tickled her senses.

"I think it's burning," Max said bluntly, drawing their attention to the wafting smoke.

Logan lunged for the stove and yanked the griddle off the burner, fanning the pungent plume with the spatula in one hand while he silenced the playlist on his phone with the other.

"I don't think you guys should be allowed to cook anymore," Max said so matter-of-factly, Abby and Logan couldn't help but laugh.

"I think you might be right." Abby grinned, sliding her arm around Max's shoulder while Logan assessed the damage.

"This side still looks good." He tapped the perfectly golden crust. "I think it's salvageable."

"Can I have the next one?" Max asked, wrinkling his nose.

"Sure thing, bud." Logan slid the burnt sandwich onto a plate and dipped a second one into a bowl of lightly beaten egg.

"What are you making?" Abby eyed the slices of ham and gruyere cheese on the cutting board.

"Monte Cristo sandwiches," Max said, stealing a slice of cheese. "I've never had one before, but Logan says they're his favorite. And I think I'll like it because it's like a ham and cheese sandwich and French toast, and I like both of those."

"You're gonna love it," Logan told him, before turning to Abby. "Hope you don't mind, but I dug into Grandma Gladys's old recipes." He nodded toward the scuffed wooden box on the counter, now flipped open. "I couldn't remember how she made 'em."

Her throat suddenly felt tight, and she swallowed. "Yeah, of course. They're yours."

Squinting, he tilted his head to the side. "No, they're *yours*. I gave them to you. Which reminds me." He reached into his pocket and pulled out a tiny brass key looped on a gold chain—the key Gladys used to guard a lifetime's worth of carefully curated recipes. "You probably don't want to leave this on the counter unless you want the whole world to discover your culinary secrets."

He dangled the key, expecting her to take it, but she didn't move. "Are you sure?" she asked in a small voice.

"Sure about what?"

She gathered a breath, steadying her nerves. "Are you sure you want me to have the recipes? They're your grandmother's legacy, Logan. They're an important part of who you are. And I don't want you to regret—"

Before she could finish her thought, he closed the gap between them with one quick stride, cupped her face with his hands, and kissed all her concerns away. She barely heard Max's *ew* of protest, too consumed by the sweet, blissful sensation of Logan's lips against hers. She'd dreamt of this moment for so long, she let herself get lost in it, savoring each infinitesimal tremor and tingle, cascading down the length of her body.

When he finally broke away, he still cradled her face, his forehead pressed to hers. "Does that answer your question?"

"Uh-huh," she murmured, deliciously dazed.

He stepped behind her and swept her hair aside, settling the key at her collarbone. The smooth metal cooled her hot skin as he hooked the clasp, letting her hair fall back around her neck.

She caressed the key with her fingertips, glancing up to meet Logan's simmering gaze. The only thing that could make the evening more complete would be a phone call from Carla, telling them she'd made a mistake and Max wouldn't be leaving after all.

"Can we eat now?" he asked, not bothering to hide his youthful annoyance at their gross kissy-face display.

"Yep." Logan tossed her a wink before turning back to the stove. "I'll try not to burn this one."

While Logan tended to the sandwiches, Max helped her set the table. And with each shared smile and mirthful laugh, she tried to reconcile how her heart could both mend and break, all at the same time.

Chapter Twenty-Seven

NADIA

A FAMILIAR DISCOMFORT wrapped around Nadia's chest, making it difficult to breathe. How could she tell Evan what happened? How could she open the door to her greatest pain and humiliation? Once he found out, would he view her differently?

She tentatively lifted her gaze, her mind grasping for ways to evade his question. But something in his expression—a softness that spoke of his genuine concern—stilled every excuse.

"My boyfriend proposed on New Year's Eve." She caught the spark of surprise in Evan's eyes. And something more—jealousy, maybe? She tucked the thought away, trying to focus. "He threw a huge party in his apartment every year and invited all his friends and family. It was a pretty big deal, and I had a feeling he was going to propose that night. Brian liked an audience."

Her pulse thrummed in her throat, fluttering like an anxious butterfly, desperate to escape. She drew in a shaky breath, forcing it back down.

"As we all watched the ball drop on TV, Brian dropped to one knee." His beaming face still haunted her dreams. So handsome. So confident. So assured. Like an actor taking the stage. He had his speech timed perfectly. The instant she'd said yes, he'd kissed her at the stroke of midnight. Celebratory cheers and confetti had swirled around them like a snow globe. She'd been so dazzled by the dreamlike moment, she'd barely had time to think.

"And you said yes?" Evan's voice held a cautious edge, as if he knew the answer and didn't like it.

She nodded, the heat of humiliation crawling up her neck as she painfully recalled what happened next. "But in the midst of celebrating, a power surge in the building shut all the lights off, plunging the room into darkness. There were squeals and laughter and chaos as everyone joked it was the end of the world." She closed her eyes at the memory. Mere seconds later, it had been. Her world, at least.

"It felt like ages until the power came back on. And while we waited, I couldn't find Brian, even though he'd been standing next to me when the lights went out." Her throat burned, and she found it difficult to swallow, almost as if she'd forgotten how.

She felt Evan's hand wrap around hers, warm and reassuring, lending his strength without a word. She opened her eyes but couldn't meet his gaze. "When the lights came back on, I saw Brian kissing another woman."

Evan's grip tensed, and she forced herself to keep going despite the tears stinging her eyes. "Her name was Sarah." Sarah the surgeon. Stunning, scintillating, sexy. She'd performed surgery on Brian's torn rotator cuff three years earlier. For all she knew, the affair could have started back then.

She could still see the look in Brian's eyes when she saw them together. Not shock or shame. Not even guilt. He had the same look he got whenever he climbed into the cockpit—the look of danger and excitement. As if he relished the risk of getting caught.

"I finally understood the expression about a deer in the headlights. I wanted to run away, but I couldn't move. I felt everyone staring, waiting. Either for me to explode or for Brian to explain. I'm not sure which."

"Please tell me someone decked him," Evan growled, gripping her hand like a vise.

"I don't think anyone knew what to do. It was as if we hoped it was merely a bad dream and we'd all wake up and it would be over." Oh, how she'd prayed for that to be true. "When Brian finally had the nerve to speak, all he said was, 'I didn't mean to hurt you.'" Her lips twisted into a bitter smile. "I'll never understand why people make horrible, selfish, hurtful decisions, and then think admitting they didn't consider your feelings somehow excuses their behavior."

"Then someone decked him. Please, tell me someone decked him," Evan repeated, fuming with anger and indignation. Not even her family had reacted this strongly.

"To be honest, I don't know if that would've helped. I wasn't angry. I was—" She hesitated, struggling to put words to her deeply buried emotions. "I was confused. I just wanted to know why. Why—" Her voice broke, and Evan squeezed her hand again. Only this time, his touch was gentle, spurred by compassion, not outrage.

RACHAEL BLOOME

On New Year's Day, while she'd stood in brokenhearted silence, Brian had blurted out all kinds of excuses. He'd panicked. He got cold feet. He'd reacted rashly, grasping for one last hurrah before he tied himself to one woman for the rest of his life. He'd given her every reason under the sun, except for the truth.

"I wanted to know why I wasn't enough," she whispered, voicing her innermost fear aloud for the first time.

A tear slid down her cheek, and she didn't bother wiping it away. She had no mascara to ruin, no makeup to smear. No willpower left to be anything but herself.

Evan gently lifted her chin, meeting her gaze. "Exactly one year ago, you gave me the hard truth. Now, it's time I return the favor. So, here it is. No man—not Brian, not me, not anyone—can define your worth. You are exactly who God made you to be. And if my opinion mattered—which it doesn't—I'd tell you that you're the most incredible woman I've ever met. I haven't been able to stop thinking about you. And part of me wants to slug your ex into the next dimension, which I may or may not have mentioned already. And the other, more selfish part wants to thank him. Because if he wasn't the biggest jerk on the planet, I wouldn't get to do this."

Evan pressed his lips to hers, slow and soft at first, then increasing in intensity when she returned his kiss, matching his urgency.

As he slid his hand around the back of her neck, pulling her closer, her tea mug tumbled into the sand, along with her closely guarded rules and reservations.

Personality tests, personal goals, and ideals, even her precious compatibility scores, all fell away.

She only cared about one thing.

Capturing the moment—with all its messy, perfect imperfections—before it slipped away.

Chapter Twenty-Eight

NADIA

NADIA BARELY RECOGNIZED the woman on her laptop screen, frozen in the tiny preview window before the video call connected.

With more natural hair and makeup, she looked less like a fashion icon and more like the girl next door. And for once, she didn't care which version other people preferred. She could be both or neither, depending on her inclination. And it wouldn't change who she was—not on the inside, where it mattered most.

She had Evan to thank for that realization.

Her fingertips instinctively grazed her lips. She could still feel the warmth and pressure of his kiss, the way his thumb traced the curve of her cheek. The memory lingered in her mind, murky and muddied, mired in her guilt.

She straightened in her seat at the small campaign desk in her suite as the dial sound ended, and a man's face replaced her own.

Varun Kumar's handsome, clean-cut features filled the screen. The epitome of outward perfection, he didn't have a single hair out of place or hint of stubble. "Good morning." His grin came easily, brightening his dark, sultry eyes. And she couldn't help noticing his smile was perfectly symmetrical. No adorable slant like a certain someone she couldn't get out of her head.

"Good morning." She returned his smile, hoping it appeared more sincere than it felt, hiding her desire to be anywhere else.

When she finally saw her aunt's text last night, she'd immediately texted back, asking to cancel the video call she'd arranged with Varun. But her aunt—either by accident or design—never returned her text. Or any of her several voice mails.

"It's so nice to finally connect." He spoke with a friendly ease she would've found charming under different circumstances. "And may I add, you are even more beautiful than your photos." His compliment, though kind, had little effect.

"Thank you." She squirmed. This didn't feel right. How could she go from kissing Evan last night to a video date with Varun the next morning?

Even though she had ended things with Evan, another wave of guilt crashed into her, drowning out Varun's remarks about the Los Angeles weather. She couldn't concentrate on his anecdotes about the Santa Ana winds when she could still see Evan's face so vividly. The hurt in his eyes still stabbed her heart, leaving a visceral mark.

"Don't do this," he'd pleaded when she'd pulled away from their kiss, scrambling to her feet.

"Do what?" she'd deflected, her pulse pounding in her ears.

"Don't run."

"This," she'd said, gesturing between them, "will never work."

"It'll work if we make it work. You and me, Nadia. We have a choice. And I choose you."

The conviction in his voice had terrified her. Because she'd wanted to believe him. She'd wanted to believe they could defy the odds. But she'd just relived what had happened the last time she'd taken a risk. It still felt too fresh. Too raw. And she didn't think she'd survive that level of heartbreak a second time.

So, she'd walked away. And Evan hadn't stopped her.

"What's the weather like in—" Varun paused, glancing toward the ceiling in his high-rise office as he searched his memory. "Blessings Beach?" he added, after a moment's thought.

"Bay," she corrected, returning to the present.

"Right. Bay. To be honest, I'd never heard of it."

"Most people haven't. But it's slowly becoming a top tourist destination. My best friend just opened an inn here."

"I'd love to visit sometime."

The thought of Varun and Evan inhabiting the same space made her shudder. At a loss for an appropriate response, she merely said, "You should. It's a lovely town."

"When are you coming home?"

The question caught her off guard. Not because it wasn't a perfectly natural thing to ask. But because, strangely, Los Angeles didn't immediately strike her as home anymore. "I plan to be back in a few days." She should be leaving today, but she couldn't leave Abby. Not with Max's departure in two days.

"I can't wait to take you on a proper date," Varun

confessed with genuine earnestness. "I've looked over the profile your aunt sent a dozen times. I can't believe how perfect you are. For me, at least." His laugh had a pleasant, jovial lilt, and she couldn't help thinking how a few days ago, she would've swooned at the sound.

He seemed perfect, too. On paper *and* in person. Everything about dating Varun made sense. And she had every reason to believe they could have a good, lasting marriage.

But how could she give him a fair shot when her heart wanted someone else?

Chapter Twenty-Nine

EVAN

EVAN ROUNDED the corner at Blessed Heart Hospital and stopped abruptly. Through the viewing window of his father's room, he witnessed something unexpected.

Bonnie Larsen sat by his father's bedside, cradling his hand in her own. Not so unusual, except her perpetually sunny countenance looked crestfallen. Heartbroken, even. And she was crying. Soft, silent tears streaked her cheeks as she studied his father's sallow features. And they weren't merely the tears of a friend.

How had he not seen it before? Bonnie Larsen was in love with his dad.

Evan stood perfectly still, processing the revelation. He supposed it made sense. They'd been close for years. And when his mother passed away, they'd grown closer. First, out of shared loss. They'd both loved his mother dearly. Plus, Bonnie knew how it felt to lose a spouse, since her husband had passed when he and Mia were teenagers.

This past year, she must've hoped they could heal from their grief together. Only his dad never even tried. Instead, he withdrew deeper into his depression with each passing day. And now, *this*.

But through it all, Bonnie had remained by his side, even now. She had staying power. And if his mom could see how fiercely she cared, she'd be happy his dad had someone like Bonnie looking out for him. If only his dad knew how much he had to lose.

Evan turned, prepared to grab a coffee in the cafeteria and give them some privacy, but one of the nurses spotted him.

"Hi, Evan. Here to see your dad?" Her obvious question carried through the open door to his father's room, and Bonnie straightened, hastily wiping her tears.

Evan suppressed a sigh, reminding himself that Helen meant well. The older, motherly woman had been a nurse for decades, and took excellent care of his dad. "How's he doing today?" He'd spent a restless night on the cot, per usual, then left to make a few more test batches of Masala Chai Taffy in preparation for tomorrow's competition. But he hadn't been able to shake thoughts of Nadia—and their earth-shattering kiss—all morning and needed to talk it out with his dad. Even if it was a one-sided conversation.

"His vitals are steady. And he did well when we tested neurological reflexes like pupillary reactivity earlier this morning. He's going to make it through this. We just need to keep the faith." She placed a reassuring hand on his shoulder.

"Thanks." It had been almost a week since the stroke. Faith was all he had left.

He ducked inside the room, and Bonnie offered her most vibrant smile, as if she hadn't been crying two seconds earlier. "Hey, sweetheart. How's the taffy coming along?"

"Great. I'll make the batch for the competition first thing

in the morning, but I made enough to sell during the festival. I think it'll be a big hit with the customers, whether I win or not."

"I think so, too. And I'm happy for you, honey. I know it wasn't easy to give up your life in LA. No regrets?"

Evan hesitated. In the year since he'd moved back to Blessings Bay, no one had ever asked him that before. Sure, he'd thought about it constantly, had mulled over all the *what ifs*. But only one repeatedly came to mind.

What if he'd sold the business to Bonnie?

"I'm glad to be home," he answered honestly, avoiding the heart of her question. "What about you? Do you ever think about moving down south to be near Mia?" He sat in the chair beside her.

"Oh, heavens no." She chuckled at the thought. "What would I do in a big city like that? I miss my daughter, of course. But the rest of my family is here." Her gaze briefly flickered to his father's face. "Did you know," she said brightly, turning back toward him, "the Belles started a prayer chain the second they heard about your father's stroke? And they've been by the hospital with baked goods and fresh coffee for the nursing staff, and have sat right here with me, nearly every day since?"

"No, I didn't." Evan's throat tightened.

"And your father's crew has kept up with all their construction projects, working extra hours to stay on track."

He had known about that and couldn't be more grateful. But as Bonnie continued to list all the ways the town had come together to support his dad—to support *him*—his gratitude overwhelmed him to the breaking point. He blinked back tears, glancing up at the ceiling to keep them at bay.

"This place isn't home because Mia was born here," Bonnie said softly. "Or because Scott and I moved here when we got married. Or because he's buried here." She dabbed the corner of her eye with her sleeve. "It's home because in all my life, I've never lived anywhere like Blessings Bay, where the people actually care about each other in sincere, actionable ways. They live out their love, even when it costs them something. And that's how you know it's real." Her gaze drifted back to his father. "Love isn't supposed to be easy. It's supposed to make you better than you were before."

"Bonnie," he said gently, wanting to tell her he knew how she felt. He wanted to give his blessing, so she didn't have to hide her feelings from him. But he didn't get the chance.

His father's hand moved.

Bonnie gasped, choking back a sob.

Evan stared in shock, his blood pumping so loudly in his ears, the deafening sound muffled the beeping of the monitor.

Had his father's hand really moved? And was it involuntary or intentional?

Was the movement a reaction to what Bonnie shared?

And if so, what did it mean? Both for his father's health *and* his heart.

Chapter Thirty

ABBY

ABBY WATCHED the festivities unfold with melancholy indifference. The white tents lining the promenade billowed gently in the breeze. Live folk music from the local band, Blessings Beats, carried above the ocean hum and seagull cries. Delicious aromas from artisan booths featuring fresh sourdough, garlic butter shrimp, and lavender lemon pie lured visitors into long lines, eager to taste the delicacies.

The Blessing in a Bottle Festival was in full swing, and everyone seemed to revel in the fun. But how could Abby enjoy the merriment when Max would be leaving tomorrow? A last hurrah didn't hold much happiness when it so clearly marked the end.

"Are you okay?" Nadia slid an arm around her shoulders, following her gaze to the picnic table where Logan sat with Max, writing their messages in a bottle.

The entire festival hinged around this one event, steeped in over a century of tradition. After the town erected a temporary barrier around the bay, people would jot uplifting messages—a handwritten blessing—on a slip of paper, stuff it inside a bottle, and toss it out to sea. The tide would carry the bottle back to shore, where someone else would retrieve the bottle and thus, receive the blessing inside.

When she first learned of the tradition, Abby couldn't think of anything sweeter. And she'd looked forward to finally participating. But now? She didn't have a single positive word to impart.

Other parents with young children gathered around the same table as Logan and Max, smiling and laughing, and a stab of envy pricked her heart. Did they realize how lucky they were simply to be together? Days came and went without altering their status quo. Without ripping them apart.

"No," she answered honestly. "And I don't know how to be okay. I should be savoring these final moments with Max, but my heart hurts too much."

Nadia squeezed her upper arm. "What can I do?"

"Tell me to snap out of it, that I need to be strong for Max."

"I don't need to tell you, Abs. You're the strongest person I know. This week, I've seen you handle one crisis after the next with grace and kindness. Today will be exactly as it should be. And when the time comes to say goodbye, you won't have any regrets, because you let yourself love wholly and completely, without a single reservation."

Abby managed a small smile, bolstered by her friend's encouraging words. But she couldn't help noticing the way Nadia's gaze drifted to the booth at the end of the promenade—the one selling taffy. Uncertainty glinted in her dark eyes.

"What about you?" Abby asked softly, studying her reaction. "When it's time for you to say goodbye, will you have any regrets?"

"What do you mean?" Nadia swiveled her back toward the booth, but not before Abby caught the flicker of sadness.

She'd been so consumed by her own internal chaos she'd barely noticed her friend's crisis of conscience. Or was it something more? Nadia claimed her efforts to help Evan stemmed from doubts about her bad review. But she recognized the look in Nadia's eyes. The look she'd glimpsed in her own reflection from the moment she'd kissed Logan—the kiss that made her heart languish in limbo, agonizing over what came next.

Was it possible that during the last several days, when she'd been desperately trying to keep the pieces of her life from falling apart, her friend had been falling in love?

"All the time you've been spending with Evan lately," Abby said slowly, struggling with how to frame her question, "it's been about more than a bad review, hasn't it?"

Nadia's shoulders sagged, and the mask slipped from her features, revealing a woman torn between two impossible choices. "I thought I had everything figured out. I had a plan."

The angst and confusion in her friend's voice was unmistakable, and Abby lamented being lost in her own worries for so long. Nadia had always been there for her, and she wanted to return the favor. "If I've learned anything over the past few days, it's that plans change. And fighting for control never works. It's like trying to subdue an ocean wave. Sometimes, we have to see where it takes us, and trust that God commands the tides." Nadia grinned at her, eyes glistening.

"What?" Abby asked, swatting the flyaway hairs the wind whipped against her face.

"You're a great mom, Abs. And I hope you won't give up on that dream, even if it can't be with Max."

A surge of emotion rose in her throat, and she glanced back at Logan and Max.

Max hadn't been a part of her plans. She'd shelved motherhood in the hidden corners of her heart once Donnie died. Truthfully, even before Donnie died, when he'd refused to consider adoption or foster care. She'd given up hope of ever experiencing the exhilarating and exhausting roller-coaster ride of raising a child.

And then Max happened. A beautiful, unexpected blessing. Did she have room in her heart for another one?

Even before the question had fully formed in her mind, she knew the answer.

The view of Logan and Max stuffing their rolled scrolls inside their glass bottles blurred as tears filled her eyes. And yet, she'd never seen the world more clearly.

"Nadia—" Before she could finish her thought, her friend nodded, smiling as she nudged her.

"Go. Be with your family."

Abby hesitated, her heart tugging in two different directions. "Are you sure? I can—"

"Go," Nadia insisted. "Write your blessing in a bottle. There's something I need to do, anyway."

Abby followed her gaze back to Evan's booth with a pretty good idea what that something might be. She leaned in for a hug and whispered, "It's terrifying, but it's worth it."

When she pulled back, Nadia met her gaze, her eyes

shimmering with understanding. "Whoever gets your message in a bottle is extremely lucky."

Abby smiled, knowing exactly what she'd write.

Don't be afraid when life takes an unexpected turn. Often, your biggest blessing is waiting just around the bend.

Chapter Thirty-One

EVAN

EVAN TRIED to concentrate on the woman asking about his new Masala Chai Taffy. It had outsold the other varieties all morning and had attracted a surge of new customers curious to try the unusual flavor, but he couldn't focus. He kept scanning the crowd for Nadia. Ever since his dad's hand moved yesterday, he'd wanted to tell her what happened—he wanted to share that his dad might be on the road to recovery. In fact, she'd been the first person he wanted to tell.

The problem? She hadn't responded to any of his calls or texts since their kiss two nights ago—the night she'd walked away. Why hadn't he gone after her?

The hard truth settled in his chest. He knew exactly why. He still felt the searing sting of Hillary's rejection burning like salt water in a fresh wound. And he'd chosen self-preservation instead of perseverance. He'd waxed poetic about putting in the work—about fighting for the kind of relationship they wanted—and he'd folded under the first wave of resistance. Not exactly a raving endorsement for the Evan Blake Boyfriend Experience.

It was time to man up. Nadia may have doubts about their staying power, but he could tell she felt the same connection he did. He just had to convince her that he wasn't going anywhere.

His pulse spiked the second he spotted her weaving through the throng toward him. Man, she looked gorgeous. And different, somehow. But it wasn't her long wavy hair whipping around her shoulders in the wind or the casual blue jeans hugging her hips to dangerous effect that struck him the most. She moved with purpose—with an inner confidence and direction. She looked like a woman who knew what she wanted. And was it his imagination, or did she want *him*?

Evan heard his own voice telling the customer that it was her lucky day—she'd won a pound of free taffy! He shoved a premium gift box in her hands, and she scuttled off in excitement. In hindsight, he probably could've shooed her away with half that amount, but he didn't care. Any price was worth two seconds alone with Nadia.

"Hey." She flashed a smile—the kind that made her dark eyes glimmer and sent his already racing heartbeat into overdrive.

"Hey." There was so much he wanted to say, but where to begin? "My dad moved his hand yesterday," he blurted, unable to stop the grin bursting across his face. "The doctors say it's a good sign."

"Evan, that's fantastic news!" She looked like she wanted to hug him, and he instantly regretted the folding table filled with taffy standing between them. "Your dad is doing better *and* you're poised to win the competition later this afternoon. I'd say the day's off to a pretty good start."

"There's one thing that would make it better." He held her gaze, and she didn't flinch. This was it—the moment that would change everything. He could feel it, as real and palpable as the warm sun beaming through the clouds. "Nadia," he said above the deafening hum of his own heartbeat.

But before he could say another word, a stranger strode toward them, calling Nadia's name and waving to catch her attention.

The man wore a slick sand-colored suit and tan driving loafers, and Evan would've bet good money the guy had a personal stylist. Slick Suit stopped next to Nadia and leaned in for a hug.

Evan winced, and not just because the guy's hand lingered on Nadia's back a little too long. Standing side by side, the two looked made for each other.

"Varun, hi. What are you doing here?"

Evan took some comfort in her tone of surprise but couldn't squelch the uneasy feeling swelling in his stomach.

Varun shot him a curious glance before turning to Nadia. An effortless smile slipped across his too-handsome face. "After our phone date yesterday, I realized I couldn't wait until next week to see you in person. Besides"—his smile broadened, revealing the kind of teeth that bought dentists a vacation home—"you did say I should visit Blessings Bay."

Nadia blushed, and Evan dug his fist into the table to steady himself. There were too many things wrong with the words coming out of Slick Suit's mouth, and Evan was sure he'd misheard. He didn't believe Nadia had gone on a date the day after their life-altering kiss, phone or otherwise. Nor did he believe they'd made plans to meet up next week. And she definitely hadn't invited Mr. Probably Owns a Maserati to Blessings Bay—*their* town.

So, why did she suddenly look so guilty?

"Nadia, who is this guy?" He studied her expression, searching for any sign, no matter how subtle, that the warning bells ringing in his ears were off base.

"This *guy*," Slick Suit said, leveling Evan with a glare he deserved, "is her boyfriend. And who are you?"

Boyfriend? Evan rubbed his jaw, wondering if the guy had actually backhanded him or if it only felt like it?

"Excuse me?" an older woman interjected. "Can I try your Masala Chai Taffy? I've heard it's divine."

"Here ya go." Evan handed her a half-pound bag without taking his eyes off Nadia. "On the house."

"Really? Wow! Thank you!" The woman hurried off, clutching her prize.

Evan waited for Nadia to refute the guy's ridiculous claim, and to his relief, she said, "Not boyfriend."

"Okay, not technically," Slick Suit amended. "But it's hard to explain our customs to an outsider." He seemed to derive great pleasure in emphasizing the term *outsider*, and shot Evan a pointed glare when he added, "Most Americans ignorantly look down on arranged marriages."

Evan missed the thinly veiled insult, too distracted by the rest of his sentence.

An arranged marriage? Was Nadia going to *marry* this guy?

The words pummeled him from all sides, like being axed by a rogue wave, leaving him winded and bruised. His gaze cut to Nadia, silently pleading. *Tell me this guy has a screw loose somewhere. There's no way what he's saying is true.*

Her pained expression told him everything he needed to know, and as Nadia opened her mouth to speak, Mia tugged on his arm.

"Hey," she cut in breathlessly, as if she'd run a mile. "Mom's been trying to reach you. Your dad moved *both* hands."

The ground beneath Evan's feet seemed to shift like loose sand. He wanted to whoop or cheer, but words wouldn't come.

Were the hot tears simmering just beneath the surface tears of joy? Or because in the same moment he'd received the best news of his life, he'd also received the worst?

Chapter Thirty-Two

EVAN

EVAN SPRINTED up the stairs at Blessed Heart Hospital rather than waiting for the elevator. As he passed each subsequent floor, his pulse pounded the erratic beat of anticipation. He'd prayed and prepared for this moment—the moment his father came out of his coma.

Right now, he needed to push all thoughts of Nadia and her potential nuptials out of his mind. His father's recovery had to take priority.

He bolted into the room, breathing heavily. Bonnie and one of the nurses stood by his father's bedside. "I came as soon as I heard. How's he doing?"

"No more movement yet," Bonnie said with poorly disguised disappointment, and Evan's optimism sputtered to a halt.

He'd foolishly expected to find his father wide awake, finally on the mend. He struggled to keep his own discouragement in check.

"But Helen says he's doing well," Bonnie added with forced brightness. "Right, Helen?"

The nurse nodded. "Recovery can be a slow process. And every patient needs to go at their own pace. We'll watch for more movement, opening of the eyes, and increased responsiveness. You two keep doing what you're doing. He'll be all right. You'll see." Helen patted Bonnie's hand before excusing herself to check on another patient.

Evan was pretty sure nurses weren't supposed to make definitive statements on a patient's recovery, but he didn't care. He was grateful for the extra dose of hope.

"You hear that, Mikey?" Bonnie told his father, settling back in her chair. "Helen says you'll be just fine. And she went to Duke University, so she knows her stuff."

Evan moved closer to his father's bedside, although he had too much anxious energy to sit still. "Sorry you had to enlist Mia to track me down. I didn't realize you'd called." He must've been so distracted by Slick Suit's unwelcome arrival he hadn't noticed the vibration in his back pocket.

"I understand, honey. It's a big day. How's the new taffy doing?"

"Great. Everyone loves it. Mia's watching the booth for me, but I don't have much left to sell."

"That's fabulous! I knew they'd gobble it up. I can't wait for your father to try it."

"Me, too," he said softly, his gaze fixed on his father's face. Was he listening to them right now? Or dreaming? Or was his mind simply blank?

"We'll make sure you get back to the festival in time for the judges to announce the winners," Bonnie assured him. "I can stay here. I don't stand a chance against your Masala Chai Taffy, anyway." She added a wink for some levity.

"Thanks, but that's the last thing on my mind." In truth,

it had slipped from his thoughts the moment he'd heard the words *arranged marriage*.

"Really? You've been talking about the competition all year. And you and Nadia have worked so hard. Surely you want to be with her when they make the announcement?"

Evan shifted his feet, and the rubber sole of his flip-flop squeaked against the linoleum. "I think there's someone else she'd rather be with at the moment." He tried not to sound too bitter. Tried and failed.

"Who?"

"Her future husband."

"She's engaged?" Bonnie bolted upright, nearly falling off her chair.

"Not exactly. I don't understand the specifics." His lips curled in a sour smile, recalling Slick Suit's remark about *outsiders*. "It's some sort of an arranged marriage situation."

"A what?" Bonnie asked, agog. "People still do that?"

"Apparently."

"Well, I'm sure they can *un*-arrange it. You two were made for each other."

"Not according to Nadia. I don't check all her boxes."

"Then her list is hooey. I've seen you two together. You make a great team."

"That's what I've been saying. Minus the hooey part." He flashed a wry grin.

"Then you need to say it again. Or louder. Or in a way she can hear it."

"I've tried. How many times should a guy say the same thing before he takes a hint?"

"That depends. How many times did you fall off your surfboard before you successfully rode your first wave?" She raised both eyebrows in a challenging arch. The woman was good.

"Point taken. But it's not that simple."

"Of course it is. You like this girl. And you can see a future with her, right?"

"Sure, but—"

"No buts. You march down to that festival and sweep her off her feet."

"What about consent? Doesn't she get a say?"

"I didn't mean to carry her off like a caveman. Just show her what we all already know. What's that thing your mom used to say? Prove to her you have *staying power*."

"You remember that?" Evan asked in surprise.

"Of course! Your mother loved telling the story of how she and your father met."

"He asked her out on the first day of freshman orientation." He smiled softly, remembering every detail, he'd heard it so many times.

"Only she'd just broken up with her high school sweetheart," Bonnie added, matching his smile.

"So Dad invited her to be in his study group instead." Evan filled in the next part of the story as they ping-ponged the remaining details back and forth.

"Which didn't exist."

"So he assembled a ragtag team more eclectic than the Breakfast Club."

"And that ignited a beautiful friendship that lasted over six months."

"Until the rest of their group didn't show up for one of their study sessions."

"And your parents spent the whole night eating Chinese, chatting about music, movies, and childhood memories."

"Dad walked her back to her dorm, asked her out again, and the rest is history."

"Just think what would've happened if he gave up after that first no."

"Must've been hard," Evan murmured, resting his fingertips on the edge of the bed, mere inches from his father's motionless hand.

"But worth it. Your parents had staying power, honey. And I've seen that same strength in you."

Evan stared at his father's still form. He looked so small, so vulnerable. Strong and powerful wasn't exactly how he would've described his dad over the past year. Not as he slowly shrank away from life and everyone in it.

Evan's hand crept closer, hovering, hesitating. It couldn't be easy to lose the one person who'd been by your side through it all, to feel so alone. Maybe his father simply needed to be reminded that he didn't have to be strong on his own?

Evan spanned the few remaining millimeters, covering his dad's hand with his own. Threading their fingers together, he squeezed, pouring his heart and soul into the simple gesture.

"I love you, Dad." The sentiment—long overdue—escaped in a raspy whisper. And as the words left his lips, he vowed, from that moment on, to use them more liberally, without reservation.

His heart warmed as he recalled one of his mother's cheesy expressions. *Real men mean what they say and say what they mean.* He'd never been one to toss I love yous around, but he could stand to say it more often.

Unbidden, his thoughts flew to Nadia—thoughts he'd tried hard to bury. It was too soon for the L-word. On a rational level, he knew that. But on a deeper level, he couldn't deny the fire burning in his chest. It blazed brighter in her presence. It fueled and spurred him to be a better man. And despite the obstacles facing them, he wanted to fan the flame.

A faint pressure against his palm yanked his focus back to the present.

His heart stopped beating.

He stared, unblinking, as his father's fingertips lightly pressed against the back of his hand.

A potent blend of shock and elation surged through him like a tidal wave, nearly knocking him over when his dad's eyelids fluttered open.

"Mike!" Bonnie half gasped, half sobbed.

But Evan couldn't speak. He couldn't even breathe.

His father met his gaze, his eyes both blurry and strangely focused. He squeezed his hand again, an unspoken promise between father and son.

They'd been given more time. A second chance. And neither one wanted to squander it.

Chapter Thirty-Three

NADIA

NADIA SIPPED HER BLACK COFFEE, oblivious to the noise of the café around her. The clinking of glasses, faint hum of the espresso machine, even the soft music—it all faded into the background behind her whirring thoughts.

She longed to call Evan, to find out if his dad was okay. Did moving both hands indicate recovery from his coma? She had no idea. And the internet browser on her phone hadn't revealed a conclusive answer. Only Evan could tell her for sure. And after what happened that afternoon, she doubted he wanted to speak to her.

She pinched her bottom lip between her teeth, tormented by the look on Evan's face when Varun taunted him with the possibility of their arranged marriage. He'd been shocked, and rightfully so. She still couldn't believe Varun had showed up, so out of the blue.

But then, a few days ago, she probably would've appreciated his assertiveness. He knew what he wanted and wasn't afraid to take action. Objectively, the man checked all her boxes. She'd given her aunt an exhaustive list, and she'd delivered on nearly every request. How would she explain sending Varun home, rejected and disgruntled? She couldn't expect her aunt to comprehend something she didn't fully understand herself.

"Pastry for your thoughts?" Sage set a white chocolate éclair on the table and took the seat across from her.

"I doubt they'd make any sense, even if I told you."

"Try me." Sage flashed an encouraging smile.

Nadia sighed. She didn't relish the prospect of spilling the messy details of her personal life, but Sage could be trusted. Plus, she'd have to confess to her aunt soon, anyway, and she could use the practice. Maybe Sage could help organize the internal chaos into something vaguely coherent?

"To put it bluntly," she said in a tone of lingering disbelief, "I finally found the perfect man, and I turned him down."

"You mean Evan?"

Startled, she fumbled her coffee cup, sloshing some of the hot liquid onto the table. She grabbed her napkin and mopped up the spill, ignoring Sage's all-too-knowing smile. "What makes you think it's Evan?"

"It's a small town. You can't change your shampoo brand without everyone knowing about it. Besides, I've seen you two together. It's obvious you have a connection."

Nadia squirmed. She wanted to believe she'd been more guarded, more in control of her emotions. But the truth was, Evan drew her out of herself in ways she couldn't explain. Being with Evan made her more open, vulnerable, and authentic. And she liked this version of herself.

"That may be true," she admitted, adding, "but I don't mean Evan. I'm talking about someone else. Someone—" She hesitated. How could she describe her relationship to Varun in a way Sage could understand? Circumventing the arranged marriage situation, she said simply, "Someone who I thought was exactly the kind of man I wanted. And he was. Except, he wasn't. And now I'm not making any sense."

"Maybe more than you think," Sage said softly, twisting the hem of her apron into a crinkled knot. "I thought I met the perfect guy once. We were only in high school, but we knew we wanted to spend the rest of our lives together. We'd made all these plans for after we graduated—plans for our future." Her normally bright sea-green eyes dimmed, shadowed by a painful memory.

"What happened?"

Sage lifted her shoulders in a shrug that said she still wasn't sure. "Sometimes, we don't know the people in our lives as well as we think."

Her words sank with a heavy weight, dragging Nadia deeper into her doubts. "That's what scares me. How can you be sure you're picking the right person?"

"Considering my track record, I don't think I'm qualified to answer that question. But the next time I like a guy—*if* there is a next time—I will take a good, hard look at his life. Does he have a habit of running away when things get dicey? Or does he stick by the people he loves?" There was a strain in her voice that spoke of a deep-seated betrayal, and Nadia hoped she'd share more of her story, even as her own thoughts drifted to Evan.

Ever-steady Evan. Based on the relationships in his life, he definitely had staying power, to borrow his mother's apt expression.

"I think the best wisdom I can offer," Sage continued, leaving her past buried, for the time being, "is to find a couple you admire and ask for their secret. Do you know someone like that?"

"My parents," Nadia responded without hesitation.

"Have you asked for their advice?"

Nadia shook her head, realizing she had an even more pressing question she wanted to ask them—one she'd been avoiding most of her adult life.

"Then that's probably a good place to start." Sage scooted back her chair and stood. "My break's over, anyway, so now's your chance." She left Nadia with a bolstering smile.

As she returned behind the counter, a yearning tugged on Nadia's heart—a yearning for friends like Abby and Sage. Even Mia, who she'd only met once, seemed to genuinely care.

Back home, all but one friend had abandoned her after the breakup. And she couldn't entirely blame them. Military wives and girlfriends formed a tight-knit club—a club where she no longer belonged. Her only other connection was more of a gym buddy. They attended the same spin class and occasionally went for a smoothie afterward, but rarely talked about anything real. She'd miss conversations like this one once she went home.

Home.... The term felt more ambiguous than ever.

Nadia slipped out her cell phone, grateful most people were outside enjoying the festival, leaving CeCe's relatively bare.

"Hi, sweetheart." Her mother answered on the first ring. "Are you on your way home?"

"Not yet." Nadia traced the rim of her mug with her fingertip. "Mom, can I ask you something?"

"Of course, *beta*. What's on your mind?"

"Why didn't you and Dad ever set me up with someone? I'm thirty, and I'm the eldest daughter. Most parents would've married me off by now, but you never even brought it up. How come?" She waited patiently as the silence stretched on for several seconds. When her mom didn't respond, she asked, "Are you still there?"

"Yes, I'm still here. Your question caught me by surprise. We thought you and your sisters would be happy to find love on your own."

"Except we haven't. Well, except for Prisha. But most of us aren't lucky enough to rear-end a doctor who finds it endearing that we crochet in rush hour traffic. Some of us need a little help. You could've set me up years ago, but you didn't."

"You weren't ready," her mother said so softly Nadia had to smash the phone against her ear to catch the last word.

"What does that mean?"

"Times have changed, sweetheart. Children have a say in these matters now. You would've given your father and me a list of criteria, just like you gave Ishani. You would've expected us to find the kind of man you wanted."

"And what's wrong with that?" Nadia felt her frustration mounting, and her mother's long pause didn't help matters.

"You're a smart woman, sweetheart. Impressively so. You've earned your success, and your father and I are very proud of you. But—" Her mother hesitated again, and Nadia wanted to scream, *Just say it.*

"But," she repeated, bathing her words in maternal compassion, "you have no idea what you truly want in a man, let alone what you need."

Nadia sat in stunned silence, gripping the phone with white-knuckled force as her mother's words crashed against her like unrelenting waves. Words she knew to be true, which made them all the more painful.

"You've always been a woman of your word," her mother added tenderly. "And if you married someone tomorrow, I know you'd commit yourself to your marriage. I'm confident you'd even create a comfortable, happy life for yourself. But strange as this may sound coming from your mother, I want more for you than a comfortable life. More than happiness, even. I want you to have a *full* life, filled with all the greatness God has for you. And that often means stepping outside our comfort zone and facing our fears. You need someone who will not only climb the mountain with you, but who can help pull you back on your feet when you're tired—who can help you reach new heights. And a man who will let you do the same for him in return."

A sweetness coated her mother's voice, as if she spoke from intimate experience. "I want you to find what your father and I share. And if that's through an arranged marriage, I'll support you. But something tells me that may not be the right path for you. And that maybe you already know what the right path is."

Tears pooled in Nadia's lashes, threatening to slip past her defenses. The whole time her mother spoke, one man came to mind. And she prayed she wasn't too late.

"Do you understand what I'm saying, *beta*?"

"Yes, Mom. I do. And, Mom"—she wiped the tears from her eyes—"I love you."

"I love you, too."

Nadia hung up the phone, knowing exactly what she needed to do.

Chapter Thirty-Four

NADIA

NADIA PUSHED through the crowded promenade toward the podium. The judges had already begun their announcements. Where was Evan? It had been hours since he left for the hospital, and she assumed he'd be back to hear the winners announced. If he won and wasn't present to collect the blue ribbon, it would go to the runner-up.

"It was a close competition this year." A short, portly man Nadia assumed to be the town's mayor spoke into a handheld microphone. "The other judges and I had a hard time narrowing it down to the top three, and we sampled each of the entries more than once."

"It's a tough job," one of the judges shouted from his position at the long folding table, "but someone's gotta do it."

This elicited laughter from the audience, and Nadia followed the sound of Verna's cheerful chortle toward the stage, where she stood near the front with the rest of the Belles.

Still no sign of Evan. Had he stayed at the hospital with

his dad? If so, she hoped that meant good news, not bad.

The mayor entertained the audience with a few anecdotes about festivals past, then complimented some of the more notable contest entries before miming a drumroll, leading to the announcement of the third-place winner.

"In third place, we have a deep-fried scallop drizzled with a garlic-sriracha aioli sauce from Hugo Ruiz, head chef at The Sawmill."

Applause erupted as Hugo took the stage to collect his white ribbon.

Still no Evan.

"In second place, we have a raspberry lemon petit four with a pink champagne glaze from CeCe Dupree, owner of CeCe's."

More applause and murmuring as onlookers oohed and aahed over the winning entries. CeCe mounted the stage to collect her red ribbon.

Each of the finalists gave a brief speech, delaying the blue-ribbon announcement, but Nadia still hadn't glimpsed Evan. Maybe he wasn't coming?

Her heart thrummed with conflicting emotions. On one hand, his father's health came first. If he'd recovered from his coma, of course Evan would want to stay with him. On the other hand, she knew how much the blue ribbon meant to him. According to the Belles, he'd obsessed over it all year. To finally win and then lose by default didn't seem fair.

Her pulse pounded in her ears as the mayor wielded the microphone. "And last but certainly not least, in first place, and winner of the beloved blue ribbon, we have an entry that was both unexpected and extraordinarily delicious."

Nadia's breath caught in her throat, trapped by anxious

anticipation. She instinctively inched closer, as if she might miss the mayor's next words.

"Let's give a big round of applause for Evan Blake of Tammy's Taffy and his tantalizing new flavor, Masala Chai."

Thunderous cheers and applause echoed around her, as if the entire town knew how hard Evan had worked to win. The mayor searched the sea of faces, expecting Evan to take the stage.

A jolt of panic zipped through her. She couldn't let him miss this opportunity, but what could she do? She spotted Mia near the front of the crowd, staring at her phone, and a burst of hope propelled her forward. "Is that Evan? Is he coming?" she asked when she reached her.

"That was my mom. She said Evan's dad came out of his coma."

"Oh, praise God!" Overcome with emotion, Nadia enveloped Mia in a hug so tight, her tears sprang to the surface. "He's okay?"

"According to the doctors, there doesn't appear to be any long-term damage. But he needs rest, so Evan's on his way over. It'll take him a few minutes to get here, though."

"Can't we just tell the judges he's on his way from the hospital?" Nadia asked. Surely, they'd make an exception for Evan given the circumstances.

"Maybe. Or you could accept the blue ribbon for him."

"Me?"

"Sure! Technically, you came up with the recipe together, anyway." Mia nudged her toward the stairs. "Go accept it on Evan's behalf, then stall until he gets here."

"Stall?"

"Give a speech." Mia grinned and gave her another little

push, as if she had no doubt Nadia could pull it off.

Nadia shuffled toward the stage, feeling less confident in her vamping abilities. She mounted the steps. The gathering looked even larger from her new vantage point.

"May I help you?" The mayor eyed her with confusion.

"I'm Nadia Chopra. I'm a—" She hesitated. How should she describe herself? "I'm a friend of Evan's," she said, settling on the most straightforward answer. "I helped him make the Masala Chai Taffy and I'd like to accept the ribbon on his behalf."

"Oh." It took the mayor a second to process the new information before he smiled warmly. "In that case, allow me to offer my congratulations." With dramatic flair, he awarded her the first-place ribbon, then led the onlookers in another ovation.

"Thank you." Nadia cradled the coveted prize, careful not to crease the silky blue material.

The mayor held the mic in front of her mouth. "Would you like to say a few words?" Nadia turned her gaze toward the crowd. Tourists and townspeople covered every inch of the promenade, standing shoulder to shoulder. She didn't have an aversion to public speaking, but for a moment, her mind went blank. "Miss Chopra?" the mayor prompted, and Nadia cleared her throat.

Just say the first thing that pops into your head.

"Many of you don't know me," she began, waiting for her brain to catch up with her words. "I'm a professional product reviewer, which is sort of like a social media influencer but more official." She cleared her throat again. Why did it suddenly feel so dry? *Just keep talking.* "A year ago, I reviewed Tammy's Taffy, and although I loved the taste and texture, I thought the owner played things a little too safe. I thought he was afraid to take risks." She smiled, realizing how much her opinion had changed. "It wasn't until I met Evan recently that I realized I couldn't be more wrong." Her thoughts swirled, replaying every moment with Evan from the past several days.

"Evan Blake is the bravest man I know." The admission spilled out of her like a floodgate opening. She barely noticed the sea of strangers, staring, gawking, hanging on to her every word. She simply let her heart do the talking. "He's not just brave because he tackles enormous waves every day, which is something I find personally terrifying. And it's not because he gave up everything in LA, uprooted his entire life, and put his family first. He's the bravest man I know because when it comes to matters of the heart, he doesn't hold back."

"That's not entirely true."

Nadia's heart stilled at the familiar voice. She turned slowly.

Evan stood on stage, a mere two feet away. How much had he heard?

"I *have* been holding back." His intense blue-green eyes peered into hers as if no one else existed. "I've let fears and doubts dictate my life for far too long." His gaze fell to the ribbon in her hands. "I've dreamt about winning this contest since my mom died. She'd been runner-up for years, and I thought winning would not only fulfill one of her lifelong dreams but would prove something to myself—prove I could run her business successfully. That I'd done the right thing taking it over. But the truth is, this ribbon can't tell me what I already know. What *you* helped me realize."

He met her gaze again, and she held her breath, desperate

for him to continue. What had she helped him realize?

"This isn't what I'm meant to do with my life. Which is why I'm selling Tammy's Taffy."

A collective gasp reverberated around the promenade, but Evan didn't seem to notice. He only had eyes for her.

"Really?" she whispered, needing him to say it again.

"I'm selling to Bonnie Larsen. She's going to incorporate Tammy's Taffy into Sweet Blessings but keep the name, in honor of my mom. It's a perfect merger, and it's an offer I should've accepted a long time ago."

"What are you going to do instead?" She kneaded her bottom lip, buzzing with possibilities, but barely daring to hope.

"I'm going to take the money from selling the business and invest in a new one." His eyes glinted with excitement. "A line of surfing products, starting with Surf Skin. Or Beach Butter. Or Rash Relief. I'm still work-shopping the name." He cracked his inviting, slanted, uniquely Evan smile. The smile she'd come to miss when he wasn't around. "So, what do you think?"

I think I want to kiss you, right here, right now.

Instead of voicing her first thought, she said, "I think it's a fabulous idea."

"I was hoping you'd say that. Because I have room on my team for one more. Someone who knows a thing or two about what consumers want. And who isn't afraid to speak her mind."

Her heart thudded against her chest. "I think I might know someone who fits that description."

"I do, too. And I'm hoping she's comfortable mixing business with pleasure because I'm crazy about her."

"You are?" Her skin felt hot as Evan took a step toward her.

She sensed every single person on the promenade staring at her, just like everyone had stared the night of New Year's Eve. Except this time, it wasn't horror and humiliation that kept her feet frozen in place. This time, there wasn't anywhere in the world she'd rather be than right here with Evan, with or without the awestruck audience.

"Nadia Chopra, I've never met anyone like you. You're strong yet soft. You're brilliant but not afraid to admit when you're wrong. You have fears and insecurities, just like the rest of us, but you're brave enough to face them." He took another step toward her, blocking out the rest of the world as he crossed the stage to stand beside her. "I'm not looking for someone perfect. Because perfect doesn't exist. But I *am* looking for someone who's perfectly *you*. And I won't settle for anything less."

He stood so close she could count the freckles scattered across his nose. How had she not noticed them before? She yearned to reach up and graze them with her fingertips but didn't dare breathe in case she burst the euphoric bubble surrounding them.

She'd heard countless compliments in her lifetime, but nothing close to *this*—nothing so pure and honest and affirming. Evan knew the real Nadia, beneath her polished veneer, and he still wanted her—*all* of her. Although she'd learned she didn't *need* his approval to be secure in her identity, the fierce fire in his eyes—the one blazing with unabashed love and longing—sent her heart soaring so high, she didn't think she'd ever come back down.

"I don't know if I'll ever have what it takes to deserve

you," Evan confessed, tenderly brushing a lock of hair from her forehead. "But I promise to show up, each and every day, and give it my best shot. If you'll let me."

Nadia's fingers swept up the smooth cotton of his T-shirt, tracing the hard contours of his chest before curving around the nape of his neck. Undeterred by the onlookers, she answered him with a kiss that came from the deepest part of her heart—the part only he'd been able to reach.

Whoops, cheers, and wolf whistles accompanied their kiss, and when Nadia finally broke away, blushing and utterly blissful, she spotted Verna and the Belles beaming at her like a gang of giggly teens. Mia jumped and fist pumped from the front row, shouting, "Go, Evan!" as if he'd scored a touch-down for their high school football team.

But where was Abby? Nadia scanned the crowd, glimpsing Logan's towering figure first. He grinned and gave her a thumbs-up before drawing her attention to Abby, who met her gaze with shimmering eyes. In one glance, Nadia felt her friend's happiness radiate across the promenade. Despite her own grief, Abby still had room in her heart for joy on her behalf. A truer friendship she'd never find. A sisterhood of the soul.

"Should we go somewhere with a little more privacy?" Evan whispered as the mayor tried to restore order to the boisterous gathering.

"Probably," she agreed with a lighthearted laugh. "Although, I'll have to get used to the whole town being involved in my personal life."

"What are you saying?" Evan gripped her hand with hopeful intensity. "You're not going home?"

"I'm saying I think I found a new one."

Chapter Thirty-Five

ABBY

ABBY STOOD ON THE BEACH, savoring the sensation of
the silky sand slipping between her toes. The setting sun
hung low in the sky, its golden rays glinting off the glass
bottles bobbing in the surf.

By her side, Logan anchored her in the present—a safe
harbor she could lean against as they watched Max amble
toward the water's edge, their bottles clinking in his arms.
He'd wanted the fun of tossing all three into the ocean by
himself, and Abby would've given him the world if she could.
If only to see his bright boyish smile as often as possible
before tomorrow.

"Do you think he'll like living with Denise?" She hadn't
been able to voice the question aloud before today, as if
avoiding the topic would make it disappear.

"It's tough to say, but I sure hope so."

"Me, too." As much as it pained her to think of another
woman raising Max, she ultimately wanted what was best for
him. Even if it meant he was better off with someone else.

"Do you think you'll still be a foster mom?" Logan's

voice carried the faint strain of someone trying to play it cool, but she could tell he was invested in her answer.

"Maybe not right away. But eventually, yes." She recalled Nadia's words from earlier that afternoon. *You're a great mom, Abs. And I hope you won't give up on that dream, even if it can't be with Max.*

Somewhere out there, another child needed a mother's love. And while her heart may be broken right now, she knew she still had more than enough love to share.

"I'm glad." Logan slid his arm around her shoulders, cradling her close against him. "You're made for this parenting gig."

"You're not so bad yourself." She smiled up at him, relishing the feel of his strong, solid body pressed against hers. Oh, what she wouldn't give to stay in this moment forever.

"It's funny. After my accident, I gave up any hope of ever having a family. And I convinced myself I was okay with it. But now..." His gaze fixed on Max as his scrawny arm launched the bottle as high and far as it could.

"Would you ever want kids of your own?" As soon as the question left her lips, she grimaced. "Sorry, that didn't come out right. What I mean is—"

"I know what you mean." Logan chuckled. "You mean a biological kid. And that's not an easy answer."

She waited for him to elaborate, her heartbeat thundering, revealing how desperately she wanted him to say yes.

"I think I would. But—" He paused, and slipping his arm from around her shoulders, he turned to face her. "There's something I haven't told you." Panic lodged in her throat, making speech impossible. She stared up at him, both eager and terrified to hear what he had to say. "I've been seeing a specialist. Every week. To see if he can cure the muscle spasms."

Relief drained from her body. That's his big secret? "Why didn't you tell me?"

"I didn't want to get your hopes up. Or mine. In case it doesn't work. The guy's good. A certified crackpot, but good. But there's still no guarantee he can fix me."

"Logan," she said softly, her voice thick with empathy. "I know you want to be healed. And I don't blame you. The muscle spasms are awful. I hate that they cause you pain, and I want you to be healed, too. But you don't need to be *fixed*." From the moment they'd met, he'd had a chip on his shoulder—this belief that his injury somehow made him less of a man. She'd tried to help him see otherwise—to see himself the way she did—but he couldn't quite grasp the truth. And it broke her heart.

He shrugged. "I guess it's semantics. But I'm not sure how I feel about having kids in my current state."

"You're right." She smiled at the flicker of surprise in his eyes, and teased, "What if the child inherited your thick head?"

He laughed a deep belly laugh. "Touché. I'd definitely prefer if our kid took after you."

All the air drained from her lungs. *Had Logan really just said* our *kid? As in, his and mine?* She wished she'd recorded the moment, to play over and over, like a favorite song.

She saw his cheeks redden, even beneath his stubble, and he cleared his throat, adorably flustered. "Is Max done with those bottles yet?" He rushed to change the subject, and she hid a grin, following his gaze toward the water.

The beach had emptied as everyone gathered on the promenade to collect their kites for Light the Night, which started in less than an hour. It should be easy to spot Max on the barren shoreline, but he was nowhere in sight.

"Max?" she called out, telling herself to remain calm.

The sun had dipped behind the horizon, dimming the sky in preparation for the stars, but still offered enough light to scan the crescent-shaped shoreline in both directions.

"There!" Logan pointed toward the cape, and Abby spotted Max's small frame scampering across the rocky formation at the base, heading farther away from shore.

"What's he doing?" Her heart vaulted into her throat as the ocean spray slathered the slippery rock surface, rendering it terrifyingly unsafe.

"I don't know. But I'll go get him." Logan took off at a sprint, flinging sand in his wake.

"I'm coming with you!" Abby scrambled after him.

They raced to the end of the beach, stopping when they reached the cape.

"Wait here," Logan commanded, climbing onto the rocks.

Abby shivered as cold mist whipped past her, courtesy of the wind-tossed waves.

"Max!" Logan shouted, making good headway.

But Max couldn't hear him over the loud crash of the waves, slapping against the cliffside.

He continued to call Max's name as he shortened the distance between them. Logan would reach him soon and bring him back to safety. It would all be okay.

Abby started to breathe a little easier, but Max's sudden, startled scream wrenched her heart from her chest.

She watched helplessly as he slid down the rockface, landing in a large crevice. Her gaze darted back to Logan, her pulse hammering as she waited for him to come to Max's rescue.

Why wasn't he moving?

The world spun out of focus as reality struck her, full force.

Max was stuck, halfway out to sea with night rapidly approaching.

And Logan had just been immobilized by a muscle spasm.

Her brain knew she should call for help, but her body responded first, hoisting her onto the rocks.

She dug her fingers into the weathered grooves, struggling to gain sure footing in her bare feet. Gathering a fortifying breath, she inched forward.

Whatever you do, don't let go.

Chapter Thirty-Six

LOGAN

A SPASM RIPPED through Logan's body, sharp and intense. His jaw clenched and he bit down harder. He could handle pain. They were old friends. It was the immobility that killed him. And this—*this* was his greatest fear.

Max needed his help, and he couldn't move.

He heard Dr. Paulson's voice echoing in his subconscious, talking him through the steps of his deep breathing technique—the one he'd secretly mocked. At the time, he'd suspected it was some kind of mind-over-matter, woo-woo mumbo jumbo, but right now, he'd try anything.

Thoroughly humbled, he followed the doctor's instructions, breathing through the misery as he dug his fingers into a crevice and dragged his body a few inches forward, scraping against the wet sediment.

After what felt like hours—but probably lasted mere seconds—he'd painstakingly maneuvered the few remaining feet until he hovered above the spot where Max had slipped. Lying facedown, he peered over the edge. Max huddled on a ledge five or six feet below, hugging both knees to his chest as the cold wind misted him with ocean spray.

"Max," Logan growled through gritted teeth. His muscles burned, but the spasm had started to dull. Often the more intense the pain, the shorter the duration. For once, he was grateful for the spine-slicing agony.

"I can't get back up," Max whimpered, trying to be brave. But Logan could hear the fear in his voice.

"Don't worry. I've got you." His words sounded staccato and strained, and not at all convincing.

"*We've* got you." Abby appeared by his side, eyes blazing, hair whipped around her shoulders in a tangled web, her clothes damp and speckled with dirt. "Are you okay?" she whispered, so only he could hear above the crashing waves.

"Peachy," he grunted, attempting a wry grin. Based on her concerned expression, it probably looked more tormented than playful.

"Grab my hand." She laced her fingers through his, squeezing tightly, and a rush of pride and admiration surged through him, combatting the pain. The woman knew how to handle herself in a sticky situation. And in moments like this one, she reminded him of a swan—stunning and delicate but a fierce force of nature when provoked.

"You stay here and ground us," she directed, "while I'll ease myself down and get Max."

A pang of apprehension shot through him. What if another spasm hit and he couldn't hold on? He shoved the thought from his mind, tightening his grip with a resolve rooted deep in his gut. With his free hand, he found a groove in the stone, and dug in, anchoring himself as Abby slid down the side.

Adrenaline and determination filled every fiber in his being, and he concentrated on controlling each breath with laser focus, just like Dr. Paulson taught him.

During one of his treatment sessions, the good doctor had also told him about a phenomenon called hysterical strength, when ordinary people performed extraordinary feats in life-threatening scenarios. He suspected the doctor had been trying to lift his spirits—like some kind of grown-up bedtime story to ward off the scary muscle-spasm monsters—but he hadn't taken him seriously... until now. Right now, Logan felt like he could lift a burning vehicle over his head. Maybe even a bus.

Using Logan's bodyweight as leverage, Abby heaved herself and Max onto the flat, stony surface beside him. They both collapsed against him, and he wrapped his arms around each of them, holding them close as relief flooded his lungs.

"I'm so glad you're okay." Abby wiped a mud smudge from Max's face. "What were you thinking climbing out here by yourself?"

Max hung his head. "I needed to get my bottle past the net, so I could get a message to my dad before I leave."

Logan's chest squeezed. Such a childlike hope—that even if he could get his bottle past the barrier, it would float out to sea and somehow find its way to his father.

"Oh, Max. I wish you would've told us." Abby reached for his hand.

"You're not mad?" Max lifted his brown eyes to meet Abby's.

"Not mad. Worried. It's our job to keep you safe."

"Speaking of safe," Logan interjected, glancing at the

darkening sky. "We still need to make it back to dry land. And we don't want to miss Light the Night, do we?"

The spasm had subsided, leaving him sore and fatigued, but he no longer felt afraid. He'd learned something vital during the harrowing ordeal—something he'd known deep down but hadn't taken to heart.

While the process may not be pretty or perfect, he could come through for his family in a pinch. And with Abby in his life, he didn't need to do it alone.

Chapter Thirty-Seven

EVAN

EVAN LACED his fingers through Nadia's, keenly aware of every infinitesimal sensation. The warm pressure of her palm. The cold chill of the night air against his cheeks. Even the gentle woosh of the waves sounded more intense, more alive. He tilted his gaze toward the stars. Dozens of glow-in-the-dark kites dotted the night sky, enhancing the celestial display.

He'd grown up attending Light the Night every spring. And when he was younger, he couldn't wait to pick out his kite and send it soaring among the others, creating a special light show, unique to Blessings Bay. Much like Max, who steered his own kite a few feet down the beach with Abby and Logan, he reveled in the magic of it all. But as he grew older, the event lost some of its allure. Maybe because he'd stopped viewing it with childlike wonder. Seeing it now through Nadia's eyes awakened all the excitement from his youth. He had a feeling he'd be viewing a lot of things in life through a new lens, and the thought thrilled him.

"I've never seen anything more beautiful," Nadia

murmured, gazing at the luminescent tableau in wide-eyed amazement.

"I have." He brushed a strand of hair away from her face, and Nadia lifted her gaze to meet his, her lips twitching.

"If they gave out blue ribbons for cheesiest lines, you'd win that, too," she teased.

"What can I say?" He flashed an unabashed grin. "I watch a lot of Jayce Hunt movies."

"I could definitely see a setting like this in one of his films." Nadia glanced from one end of the beach to the other. With the kites overhead, and crackling fire pits dotting the shore, the entire bay glowed against a backdrop of dark sky and black water.

"If this were a movie, we wouldn't be observers. We'd have to fly one of the kites ourselves." He waved at Mia, who waited nearby, flying a large blue butterfly with rainbow-colored LED lights on the wingtips. On cue, she carefully passed him the winder, making sure the kite stayed aloft. Once he had control, she tossed him a wink and sauntered off to join Sage and CeCe by the fire pit.

Subtle, Mia. Really subtle.

He stole a glance at Nadia, but she didn't appear to notice, too fixated on the way the butterfly dipped and dove, dancing above them in a kaleidoscope of color.

"It's mesmerizing." She gathered her hair with both hands, securing it in a tight braid, so it didn't obstruct her view.

For several minutes, they stood side by side, their backs to the wind, watching the hypnotic performance. Evan's heart-beat quickened with each passing second, wondering when she'd spot the surprise.

"What's that?" she finally asked, squinting at the sky.

"What's what?"

"That thing tied to the string." She pointed halfway up the line. "See, it's bobbing around in the wind."

"Let's check it out." Hiding a smile, he dropped the winder at his feet and pulled the line, hand over hand, until the kite flopped into the sand. After he untied the foreign object, he carried it over to Nadia, his breath lodged somewhere between his throat and his lungs. "Here it is."

"Is that—" Nadia glanced from the item in his hands to his face, then back to his hands, trying to make sense of what she saw. "Is that a *pine cone*?"

"It appears to be."

"And is that a green ribbon?"

"Assuming my preschool teacher correctly taught me primary colors, I'm going to say yes. Yes, it is."

Nadia laughed, her dark eyes shimmering. "Evan Blake, are you asking me to the Timber Ball?"

"Is it that obvious? I was shooting for an invitation with some *nuance and originality*." He struggled to keep a straight face as he playfully evoked the words from her infamous review.

She laughed again, and the lilting sound washed over him like a refreshing wave—one he wanted to ride repeatedly, for the rest of his life.

Her beautiful lips curved upward in a smile both teasing and distractingly tempting. "I'd say you're close to successfully executing a *sensory-dazzling experience*." She echoed her words from the same review, inching toward him.

"Only close?" His heart stopped beating the second she placed her hand on his chest.

"There's one sense missing." She closed her eyes, tilting onto her tiptoes.

As their lips met, he tasted hints of spicy chai and sweet taffy and undertones of something richer—something extraordinary. If love had a flavor, it would taste exactly like this.

As soon as the corny thought crossed his mind—and surpassed even the most ludicrous line from one of Jayce's cliché-riddled chick flicks—reality lit up like a neon sign.

Somewhere between bad reviews and blue ribbons, he'd fallen hard for this woman. Wholly, completely, undeniably in love. And he knew the perfect way to show her.

Chapter Thirty-Eight

ABBY

ABBY PAUSED in the doorway between the kitchen and dining room, the straight-from-the-oven casserole steaming in her hands. Her found family—plus one extra—sat around the table. Logan, Max, Nadia, Verna, Carla, Sage, and Serena sipped freshly squeezed orange juice and piping-hot coffee, waiting for her culinary pièce de résistance—the recipe she hoped would become her signature breakfast item.

Her heart thrummed with nervous anticipation as she set the dish on a trivet at the head of the table and served Logan first. She slid the heaping slice onto his plate, watching his expression closely as the fragrant steam tendrils curled toward him.

"Abs, this smells incredible." He closed his eyes, inhaling the sweet and savory scent.

"Try it and tell me what you think," Abby urged, too anxious to wait until everyone else had been served.

Logan shot her a curious glance, then dug his fork into the plump layers of battered bread, glazed ham, and melted cheese.

Abby held her breath, clasping her hands together to still their nervous jittering as he took his first bite.

"Oh, wow." He released a low growl of approval while he chewed. "This is the best thing I've ever tasted." To punctuate his point, he immediately dove in for another forkful.

Abby beamed as if he'd just awarded her the Nobel Prize.

"Do the rest of us get to try it?" Nadia cut in playfully, followed closely by Max, who added, "Yeah, I'm starving. And it smells really good."

He held his knife and fork in each hand, propped on the table like goal posts, and Abby's heart lurched. This would be their last meal together before Denise came to take him away. She swallowed the lump of sadness stuck in her throat, determined to keep her emotions in check.

While Logan devoured his first helping, eager for his second, she served the rest of the table, treasuring each exclamation of delight and utterance of praise. But when it came time for Serena's turn, her confidence faltered.

Serena eyed the unusual casserole, appearing particularly put off by the topping. "Is that powdered sugar? And"—she dipped the tines of her fork into the pinkish-red sauce Abby had artfully drizzled over the top—"some sort of raspberry preserve?"

"It's a homemade raspberry sauce." Abby's heart sank at the crinkles in Serena's nose.

"And it's divine!" Verna declared with a flourish.

"I agree," Carla added from across the table. "I've enjoyed everything you've ever made, Abby. But you've really outdone yourself this time."

Abby smiled, grateful for her kind words. And for her calming presence. While Carla might legally need to be present to help facilitate the transition, her presence was welcomed. Over the last few months, she'd become a friend. And Abby couldn't have asked for a better caseworker. Carla had recognized that while their situation was unorthodox, it was the right fit for Max. And she'd helped them walk through the steps necessary to make it happen.

"It tastes kinda familiar but better. It's hard to describe." Logan reached for the serving spoon, helping himself to another slice.

"I was thinking the same thing." Sage licked her fork tines, squinting as she mulled over the possibilities. "But I can't quite put my finger on it."

"Same here," Nadia agreed. "What's your secret, Abs?"

"I'm calling it a Monte Cristo Casserole, and it's inspired by Logan's grandmother's sandwich recipe."

While her friends praised her culinary creativity, Abby couldn't tear her gaze from Logan's. He held so much love in his eyes, as if it meant the world to him that she'd used the recipe box, blending their lives together by bringing his past into her future. She'd been so afraid to cross that line in the sand, but now, she didn't want to hold back, not even for a second. And she couldn't wait to see what came next.

"How interesting." Serena's skeptical tone drew Abby's attention. But as the finicky woman daintily dug her fork into her labor of love, Abby realized she no longer cared what she thought. She'd tried her best to give Serena a pleasant stay, and that would have to be good enough.

Apart from Max, who ate his breakfast with unconcerned gusto, a collective hush settled across the table. All eyes turned to Serena, watching in anticipation as she chewed her microscopic bite as slowly as humanly possible.

She swallowed, her expression unreadable. "It's—" Serena hesitated, as if searching for the right word. "It's certainly... unexpected." She paused again, this time bestowing a surprising smile. "Delightfully and deliciously unexpected." She sank her fork back into the pillowy layers. "I agree with Logan. It's one of the best breakfast casseroles I've ever had."

"Hear! Hear!" Nadia raised her glass of orange juice in a toast. "To Abby, a culinary genius, and her new signature dish, the Monte Cristo Casserole."

Abby blushed as everyone applauded, and for the remainder of breakfast, she managed to enjoy her time with friends and family, rather than agonizing over the seconds ticking away until Denise arrived.

It wasn't until it came time to clear the table that Abby's heartache returned. In mere minutes, they'd have to say goodbye. And she wasn't sure she could find the words.

"Abby," Serena said softly, finding her alone in the kitchen. "May I speak to you in private for a moment?"

"Of course." Abby set the last lemon pistachio scone in the Tupperware container and secured the lid.

Serena shifted her feet and glanced toward the ceiling as if looking for her nerve. "I don't quite know how to ask you this."

"Straight and to the point is usually best," Abby offered kindly, fairly confident she knew what Serena was about to say.

Serena met her gaze with contrition in her eyes. "I know I haven't been the easiest guest." She paused, and Abby didn't refute her point. "And before I go any further, I have to be honest with you. I've already written my review."

Abby's pulse quickened, but she waited for Serena to fill the silence.

"I didn't want to ask you for a favor under false pretenses or with contingencies. I've already scheduled the review to go live by 10 a.m. tomorrow morning. By the time you read it, I'll be gone. So, my request comes without any strings attached. And you have every right to refuse, without any negative repercussions."

As reality settled, so did a surprising sense of calm. The review was done. It would be out in the world tomorrow, and there wasn't a single thing she could do apart from accept it and move forward. After all, she'd overcome far worse than a bad review.

To her astonishment, she found herself smiling. "Serena, would you like to stay another night so you can attend the Timber Ball with Zander?"

Relief flooded Serena's features. "How did you know?"

"That's the thing about a small town. We're like family. Few things escape our notice. Do you have a dress?"

"No. I figured I'd drive to one of the larger cities this afternoon to find one."

"No need for that. You can borrow one of mine." Abby removed her apron and set it on the counter.

Serena's eyes widened. "I couldn't do that."

"Of course you can. My late husband was in the Air Force. I've been to more military balls than I can count. I'd love for some of my beautiful dresses to be put to good use." She headed for the hallway and waved for Serena to follow. "Apart from you being a few inches taller, we're almost the same size. I'm sure we'll find something that'll fit."

"I don't understand." Serena stood stock-still, visibly

stunned. "After how I've treated you, why are you being so nice to me?"

Abby surveyed the space around them—her home. "Do you know why I started this inn?" Serena shook her head. "When I first came to Blessings Bay, I'd lost everything. But this town gave me a new life. It gave me a family. And that's a gift I want to extend to every single person who steps through that front door. We may have started off on the wrong foot, Serena. But I still want you to feel like family. And that's not going to change because of one bad review."

Serena's eyes glistened with unshed tears, and for the first time, Abby glimpsed the broken woman behind the flawless facade.

Maybe there was more to the Savvy Sojourner than met the eye?

Chapter Thirty-Nine

ABBY

ABBY SHIVERED IN THE DRIVEWAY, despite the pleasant afternoon air. How could the sun shine so brightly when internally, storm clouds gathered?

Logan lifted Ron's hutch into the trunk of the black SUV and lowered the hatch. Abby flinched at the finality of the loud, caustic *click* as it closed.

"He'll be okay in the back all by himself?" Max strained to see through the tinted windows, swaying onto his tiptoes from where he stood on the curb.

"He'll do great," Logan assured him. "I stuffed towels around the sides, so it won't shift."

"And I'll drive carefully," Denise added, slamming the rear door after she'd loaded Max's duffel bag. A forced smile stretched across the woman's face. She'd been antsy and impatient from the moment she arrived half an hour ago, and Abby couldn't figure out why. "Well," Denise said briskly, "time to say goodbye."

Abby winced at her curt, careless tone. Didn't she realize how hard this was for all of them?

"Here. I'll help you with that." Denise yanked Max's backpack off his arm and flung open the front passenger door, tossing it onto the seat.

Abby decided to ignore the woman's callous behavior, and knelt on the curb, focusing all her attention on Max. "We're going to miss you so much."

He flung his arms around her neck, and she hugged him tightly, never wanting to let go. Tears burned her eyes, and she felt Logan's hand on her shoulder, offering support. At that moment, she was grateful Carla and the others had said goodbye to Max inside. She wanted to stay in this bubble forever—just her, Logan, and Max.

"You'll come see me?" he murmured against her hair.

"Of course."

"And Logan, too?"

"You won't be able to get rid of us." Logan dropped to one knee and wrapped them both in his strong, reassuring embrace. "We'll bug you so much with visits and phone calls, we'll be like those barnacles that grow on whales and look like warts."

"Ew. Gross." Max snickered, his sadness momentarily forgotten, and Abby's heart swelled with affection for the man kneeling beside her. He was an incredible dad.

"Hey. What are you doing?" Logan's gruff tone caught her off guard, and she glanced up in surprise.

Logan sprang to his feet, and Abby followed his gaze to where Denise stood by the car, rummaging through Max's backpack.

Denise tensed, her eyes widening as if she'd been caught red-handed. "I'm just making sure Max has everything he needs for school."

RACHAEL BLOOME

Something about her tone and posture sent Abby's warning bells blaring. Logan must've had the same suspicions because he stepped toward Denise, hand outstretched. "Give me the backpack."

Denise glanced between them, as if assessing their collective threat. Her jaw set with defiance. "One second." She returned to her rummaging.

"Give me the backpack, Denise," Logan growled, taking another step toward her.

"I just have to—there!" Denise cried in triumph. She yanked a nondescript composition notebook from among the jumble of loose papers, binders, and books.

"What's that?" Logan demanded.

"Nothing." Denise clutched the notebook to her chest, her eyes flashing. She looked almost crazed.

Abby tugged Max closer to her side.

"Hand it over." Logan jutted out his palm.

"Here. Take it." Denise tossed the bag at Logan, and he caught it by the strap.

"And the notebook." He kept his voice steady, but Abby heard the agitation building.

The woman gripped the notebook tighter and darted her gaze toward the driver's seat. Was she really contemplating a hasty getaway? What on earth did Denise want with a child's notebook? None of this made any sense.

Denise dug her keys out of her purse and backed away, stumbling off the curb. Her keychain clattered to the pavement, and Logan dove for it before Denise had time to react.

"Those are mine!" she snarled like a feral cat.

"And the notebook belongs to Max. I'm happy to trade." He dangled the keys in front of her face, and she glowered.

While Abby had no idea why the woman wanted the notebook so badly, she silently thanked Logan for standing his ground. There was clearly more to the story—and Denise—than they realized.

Abby waited in breathless silence for the woman's next move, Max tucked safely against her side. Surely, without her keys, Denise would give up and surrender the notebook.

"You don't want to do this." Denise narrowed her eyes into vicious slits and slipped her hand inside her purse. A second later, she pointed a Taser at Logan's chest.

Abby's heart vaulted into her throat, and she yanked Max backward onto the lawn before grabbing her phone from her back pocket.

"No cops," Denise snapped, brandishing the Taser. "Just give me the keys, and I'll disappear. You can keep the kid."

The derisive way she spat *You can keep the kid* dragged all of Abby's anger to the surface. "As if we'd let you take him anywhere now."

"What about Ron?" Max asked in a soft, scared voice.

"It's going to be okay," Abby assured him, trying to keep calm despite her reeling pulse. "Why do you care so much about Max's notebook?"

"That's none of your business. Just give me the keys and no one has to get hurt." She kept the Taser aimed at Logan's torso.

"I hate to break it to you," Logan said with surprising nonchalance. "But you wouldn't be the first woman to tase me. Not even the first woman in present company."

If she hadn't been so terrified, Abby would have laughed. The first time they met, she'd accidentally zapped Logan, mistaking him for an intruder. She'd felt awful about it at the

time, and she certainly didn't want to see it happen to
him now.

Denise darted her gaze between them in confusion,
clearly rattled. "Just give me the keys!" she shrieked, coming
unglued and horrifyingly unpredictable.

Fear gripped Abby's chest, both ice cold and burning
hot. She wanted to scream for help, torn between protecting
Max and rushing to Logan's side.

They'd pushed Denise too far, and from the unhinged
glint in her eyes, she was capable of anything.

"Abby, take Max inside," Logan said as calmly as possible,
but she caught an undercurrent of uncertainty that sent a
chill down her spine.

She grabbed Max's hand, desperate to keep him safe, but
plagued by the thought of leaving Logan alone with this
maniac.

What should she do?

A wailing siren echoed down the street, and Abby's fear
gave way to relief as a squad car sailed toward them, lights
blazing.

How did they—? Abby glanced over her shoulder to see
Verna peeking between the curtains.

The woman had a gift for sussing out scandal, and for
once, Abby couldn't be more thankful.

Chapter Forty

NADIA

"I can't believe it," Nadia breathed, still in shock.

"Neither can I." Abby stood beside her near the front window, her gaze fixed on Logan and Max, cross-legged on the sitting room floor. Ron snuggled in Max's lap, contentedly nibbling all the fresh carrots and celery Max offered him as conciliation for the recent traumatic events. Not that Ron understood what happened. Nadia barely understood it herself. Even after Abby spent the last half hour trying to explain it to her.

"So, this whole time," Nadia echoed, trying to make sense of it all, "Max had a notebook filled with credit card and social security numbers?"

"And names, dates, and other personal identification information. Although, it wasn't *filled*. Just a few pages near the back. But enough to be worth a lot of money to the wrong people."

"Why did Max have it? And why didn't he ever say anything about it?"

"He had no idea what he had. He needed a notebook for school, and when the Hobarts wouldn't give him one when he asked, he decided to borrow it. A day or two before they skipped town. By the time they realized what had happened, the cops had already emptied their place and were looking for them. They couldn't come back."

"So, they sent Denise to... to what? To find out if Max had it?"

"They figured it was the most-likely explanation. They'd been careful to pack everything they needed, and when they realized the notebook was missing, they knew it hadn't walked away on its own."

"But pretending to be related..." Nadia shook her head in disbelief. "That's deceitful on a whole other level."

"I know. According to her police statement, she figured that would be the best way to get close to Max without arousing suspicion. The cops were on high alert for any sign of the Hobarts or any accomplices returning to Blessings Bay."

"But how did she do it? How'd she pull it off without Carla or anyone else figuring it out?"

"Apparently, after decades of stealing people's identities, you get pretty good at it. Denise Smith is a real person. She just isn't the person we met."

"That's downright evil." Nadia still had trouble wrapping her head around a plot that nefarious. "Didn't you say she had a photo of Max?"

"The Hobarts took it. Carla said they had quite a few on their phones, according to the original caseworker, who resigned for obvious reasons. She said it's common for some of the worst foster parents to take staged photos. That way, if their motives are ever called into question, they have supposed evidence that they're taking care of the child."

"That's awful."

"It is. And luckily, it doesn't always work. Carla said Max's original caseworker didn't do his due diligence and ignored a lot of red flags."

"Poor Carla. She must feel terrible about Denise." Nadia's heart went out to the woman, who, as far as she'd seen, genuinely cared for Max.

"She does. And it wasn't her fault. I thought something felt off about Denise, but I never said anything." Tears welled in Abby's eyes, and Nadia rushed to reassure her.

"It's not your fault, either, Abs."

"Maybe not. But when I think about what could've—" Abby's voice caught, and Nadia had a feeling she knew what her friend had been about to say. She'd been wondering the same thing all afternoon. Did Denise plan on taking Max with her? Or would she have run off with the notebook, leaving Max behind?

An icy chill ran through Nadia's veins at the terrifying thought. For all their sakes, it was best to put the ordeal behind them. "Max's safe now. And he's not going anywhere. We should focus on that."

"You're right." Abby sniffled, smiling through her tears. "And he's not the only one who's staying." She turned her glistening eyes on Nadia. "You're really moving to Blessings Bay?"

"What can I say? I think I finally see what you love about this place."

"It is pretty special, isn't it? And you'll survive without your fancy clothing boutiques?"

"It'll be hard," Nadia said with a laugh, "but worth it."

Abby threw her arms around her, squeezing all the air from her lungs before she took a step back, wide-eyed. "Wait. What are you wearing to the Timber Ball tonight?"

"One of my sundresses, I guess. I don't have time to go shopping."

Abby blinked, as if she'd misheard. "You're going to wear a casual sundress to a black-tie event?"

Nadia shrugged. "I know it's hard to believe coming from me, but I genuinely don't care what I wear. I just want to be with Evan." She imagined dancing in his arms, swaying to a tune only they could hear, and her cheeks flushed.

Abby's eyes swam with tears again, and she pressed both palms to her heart, practically swooning.

"Don't start planning our wedding just yet," Nadia teased. "You and Logan need to walk down the aisle first."

Now, it was Abby's turn to blush. "He did say something about *our kids* yesterday."

"See. I told you that you didn't have anything to worry about. That man adores you."

"He does, doesn't he?" Abby's misty gaze traveled back to Logan, brimming with unbridled affection.

"Are you sure you two don't want to attend the ball tonight?" Nadia figured they could find someone to stay with Max for the evening.

"I'm positive," Abby answered without a second of hesitation. "The only place I want to be is right here." Drying her eyes again, she turned to face her. "But I wish we wore the same size. I know you don't mind, but I would love for you to have something nice to wear."

"I know you would. And I appreciate it. But honestly, I'm okay being underdressed for once in my life." Nadia surprised herself with her own sincerity. While it would be nice to blow Evan away with some knockout gown, she knew he'd still make her feel like the most beautiful woman in the room.

Before Abby could further lament her dress dilemma, a knock at the door drew her attention. Nadia followed her into the entryway to find Verna standing on the stoop wearing the biggest grin. Even Bing—with his tongue lolling to one side—appeared to be smiling.

"Special delivery." Verna breezed through the doorway brandishing a garment bag. "For you, dear."

Nadia stepped back in surprise. "Me?"

"There's a note here somewhere." Verna glanced around the room as if it might magically appear. "Oh, that's right." She stooped and slid the envelope from beneath Bing's collar. "Here it is." She unloaded the garment bag and note into Nadia's arms.

"I—I don't understand. What is this?" Nadia stared blankly at the unexpected bundle.

"I believe that's what the note is for." Verna's eyes danced with a teasing glint.

"Open it!" Abby nudged her in excitement.

Bewildered, Nadia slipped the card from the envelope and flipped it open.

I thought you might need a dress for tonight. This one belonged to my mom. I asked Verna to do a few alterations. I hope it fits.

There was no signature on the note, but Nadia didn't need one. Her heart swelled. "It's from Evan."

Abby clapped her hands together, bouncing on her toes in breathless anticipation. Nadia would've laughed at her girlish exuberance, except she was still too dumbfounded. With tentative fingers, she grasped the zipper of the garment bag and pulled slowly. The ever-increasing *purr* matched her accelerating pulse as the zipper gave way, revealing the most vibrant royal-blue silk she'd ever seen.

"Oh, Nadia!" Abby gasped. "It's gorgeous."

Nadia slipped the gown from the garment bag, awestruck by the slender, off-the-shoulder silhouette. Delicate crystal beads dotted the fitted bodice, and tears welled as images of her mother's dupatta sprang to the surface.

"You don't like it?" Verna frowned, mistaking her tears for disappointment. "I removed some of the ruffles and bows along the neckline and hips to bring it out of the eighties, but I brought my sewing kit in case it needed a few more alterations. Your waist might be a smidge smaller than Evan's mother. And I may need to bring the hemline up an inch or two. But anything else you want changed, simply say the word, and I'll work my magic." Verna waved a small tin and the contents clinked inside.

"Thank you, but that won't be necessary. It's perfect," Nadia murmured, embarrassed by her sudden burst of emotion.

"Then why the tears, dear?"

"It's nothing. It's just—" She paused, unsure how to explain the intense, out-of-the-blue longing for something she'd tried to forget. "I suddenly had this memory from my childhood. My mother had this bright-blue dupatta that looked similar to this dress. And for some reason, I wished I had it with me." It sounded small and silly as she said it aloud. And Abby and Verna probably had no idea what she was talking about. "A dupatta is kind of like a shawl," she explained.

"Oh, I'm quite familiar," Verna said with a knowing smile. "And I have something you might like to see."

Chapter Forty-One

NADIA

"WHERE DID IT COME FROM?" Nadia traced her fingertips along the soft purple silk.

"India. My Harold and I were never blessed with children, so we traveled the world instead. I've been to thirty-nine countries, but India holds special memories."

Nadia draped the luscious fabric around her shoulders, marveling at the striking contrast of vivid blue and violet hues.

"You look like royalty." Abby's voice dripped with awe.

Still amazed herself, Nadia angled left and right, studying her reflection in the antique standing mirror in her suite. Thanks to Verna's seamstress skills, the dress fit like a dream. And the dupatta elevated the ensemble to stunning effect. She wore her hair in a simple updo with subtle makeup and jewelry, letting the brilliant colors of the dress and dupatta complement her natural beauty.

"I do feel like a princess," she admitted, smiling on behalf of her younger self.

"Evan's going to pass out when he sees you." Abby grinned.

"You think so?" Nadia's heartbeat quickened as she imagined the look on Evan's face when he saw her in his mother's dress for the first time. Would he be pleased?

The doorbell rang.

"Time to find out!" Abby sang with excitement. "But hang on. I'll be right back." She darted out of the room, and Nadia turned to Verna.

The older woman gazed at her with grandmotherly affection, ignoring Bing, who'd commandeered one of Nadia's slippers.

"Thank you for letting me borrow this." Nadia gently tugged the dupatta tighter around her bare shoulders. The silk felt cool and airy against her skin.

"My pleasure, dear. You look breathtaking."

Nadia let her eyes speak her thanks, her heart too full of love and gratitude for words. "Don't you need to get ready for the ball, too?"

"Oh, I have plenty of time for that. I like to arrive fashionably late."

Nadia hid a smile. Verna had a quirky style all her own, and she couldn't wait to see what she'd wear tonight.

Abby burst back into the room, clutching two pairs of shoes. "We may not be able to swap dresses, but at least our feet are the same size. Will one of these work?" She dangled the heels for Nadia's inspection—one pair ivory, the other black. "They're not designer brands, but they'll survive a night of dancing without blisters."

"They're perfect, thank you." Nadia selected the black strappy heels and slipped them over her bare feet before casting one last glance in the mirror. She could still hardly believe her own reflection.

"Your date is waiting downstairs." Abby's eyes sparkled with eagerness, as if Nadia had a surprise in store.

Her heart fluttered as Abby ushered her toward the stairs, purposely lingering a few steps behind.

Evan stood at the bottom of the staircase, and the moment he spotted her, the earth stopped spinning. And not because he wore the look of a man utterly besotted.

She stopped on the last step, gaping in shock. "You're wearing a tie?"

"Stunning and astute," he teased, still drinking in her appearance with admiring eyes.

"But you said you'd never wear a tie. Not even on your wedding day."

"I did. But then I realized, some people are worth stepping outside your comfort zone." He met her gaze and smiled —his slow, scintillatingly askew smile—and she slipped her arms around his neck, kissing him with zero regard for the audience behind them.

When she finally pulled back, Evan was grinning again. "For a kiss like that, I'd wear a tie every day."

"And sacrifice your ability to breathe?" She stroked the silver-striped silk that paired perfectly with his new suit, enjoying the intimacy of being eye level thanks to the added height of the bottom step.

"Oxygen is overrated."

Smiling, she tugged the tie, drawing his lips to hers once more. Was it possible his kiss tasted sweeter each time?

"Hey, lovebirds. There's a child present." Logan's playful

tone carried from the adjacent sitting room. "And don't you have a dance or something?"

Nadia laughed, too blissful to feel an ounce of embarrassment. "He makes a valid point."

"True," Evan agreed. "Although, I think he has ulterior motives for getting rid of us."

Nadia glanced over her shoulder at Abby, who blushed. Once Max went to bed, she had a feeling Abby and Logan might share a kiss or two themselves. And Nadia couldn't be more thrilled about her friend's happily ever after.

There was just one black cloud in an otherwise flawless sky—Serena's impending review.

And it was time Nadia had a word with the Not-So-Savvy Sojourner.

Chapter Forty-Two

NADIA

LATER THAT EVENING, Nadia found Serena in the ladies' room, reapplying her lipstick.

"Hi." Serena smiled when she glimpsed her in the mirror. "Can you believe this place looks even more beautiful than when we came for dinner the other night?"

"They did a wonderful job." The Sawmill had transformed their main dining room into a springtime spectacular with fragrant floral garlands draped around every window and doorway. They even hung from the ceiling and chandeliers. Refreshment tables overflowing with drinks and desserts lined the deck where they'd sat four days ago, offering a moonlit respite for partygoers in need of a break from the dance floor. The whole evening was magical, but Nadia wouldn't be able to fully immerse herself until she talked to Serena.

And apparently, she wasn't alone in her sentiment.

Serena placed the cap back on her lipstick and slipped it inside her clutch. Turning to face her, she said, "I owe you an apology. And Abby. But since you're here, I'll start with you first." She gathered a deep breath, filling her lungs with the courage to continue. "I get the feeling you don't like me very much. And to be honest, I don't blame you. I haven't really liked myself lately."

Nadia blinked in surprise. This wasn't at all how she'd expected the conversation to go.

"I sort of lost myself this year," Serena admitted, her voice strained with sadness. "I'd always loved my job, but after a while—after all that traveling, never feeling settled or having a place to call home—I felt so disconnected. So lonely. I drifted further away from my passion, my purpose. And nothing seemed to matter anymore." Regret glinted in her eyes. "That's when VRP Investments contacted me."

"Who are they?"

"They're a holding company. They own stock in hundreds of businesses around the world, mostly in the hospitality industry, ranging from huge resorts to boutique hotels to quaint bed-and-breakfasts. They wanted to hire me as an in-house reviewer."

"What does that mean, exactly?" Nadia asked, although she had an inkling she knew the answer.

"I'd continue my brand as the Savvy Sojourner as if nothing had changed, except I'd review their properties exclusively."

"And, I assume, they'd all be raving reviews?"

Serena dropped her gaze to the hardwood floor, her cheeks flushed with shame. "I said no, at first. But they doubled their offer. And I convinced myself that in the grand scheme of things, it wasn't a big deal. People follow me for travel tips. They're not asking me for political or financial advice or anything life-altering."

Her words were laced with regret, and Nadia tried to find some compassion buried deep down, behind her indignation. Serena wouldn't be the first influencer to sell her integrity to a soulless corporation.

"Moral gray areas aside," she said, trying to fit the pieces together, "that doesn't explain what you're doing here in Blessings Bay—at Abby's."

Serena tugged the bodice of her pink chiffon gown, as if she suddenly found it too snug to breathe. "Right. And that's where the gray area becomes more of a muddy brown."

"What do you mean?" Nadia's pulse spiked with apprehension. She had a feeling she wouldn't like Serena's response.

"I said I'd accept their offer, but I'd already agreed to review Abby's inn, and I asked if they'd like me to cancel." She swallowed, staring at the floor again.

"And what did they say?" Nadia prompted, her heart pounding.

"They said I should still come, but..." She paused, wincing as she added, "They told me to write a negative review."

Anger rose in Nadia's chest, and she mentally counted to ten, winding herself down.

"I know it's unconscionable," Serena continued, her features contorted with contrition. "And I should have refused. Especially when they said periodically giving another property a negative review would add credibility to all the positive reviews I'd write for them." Tears of remorse welled in her eyes. "I knew it was wrong, but I convinced myself if I chose to review places that *deserved* criticism, it wouldn't be as unethical. That's why I arrived early. I was counting on Abby not being ready for me."

A tear slid down Serena's cheek, and she roughly brushed it aside, but Nadia's sympathy vanished. She'd heard of sellouts and shady deals, but this? This trumped them all. "I don't know what to say."

"You don't have to say anything. What I did was inexcusable. And I wouldn't blame you for not forgiving me. I don't deserve it. Especially since Abby has been nothing but nice to me."

"Does Zander know about this?" Nadia couldn't imagine he'd be too keen to date someone so diabolical.

"He does. I told him everything. Including the fact that I've since turned down VRP's offer. And I've recommitted to writing honest reviews. I won't be swayed. Not when it comes to writing negative reviews *or* positive ones. From now on, it's nothing but one hundred percent honesty. No matter what."

"What about Abby's review?" Did Serena have this epiphany before or after she wrote it?

"It's the truth. And until it goes live on my website tomorrow, that's all I can say."

Nadia wanted to protest—to push for a more definitive answer. But she could tell Serena wasn't going to budge. She had no choice but to wait.

Chapter Forty-Three

ABBY

ABBY HIT refresh for the hundredth time, but Serena's review still hadn't posted on her website. "Come on, come on!" She continued to click refresh on her laptop as if her life depended on it. And in a way, it did. At least, her *professional* life.

"It's after 10 a.m. Where is it?" Panic used her stomach as a punching bag, and she suddenly regretted the second stack of pancakes.

"Take a deep breath." Nadia sat beside her on the couch, offering her moral support. "It's only 10:01. There could be a slight delay."

"It'll show up any second." Logan squeezed her hand, and she leaned into him, grateful to have all the important people in her life present for the crucial moment.

Logan and Nadia sat by her side, while Evan, Sage, Verna, and the Belles scattered around the sitting room, occupying the love seat and twin armchairs while Max played on the floor with Ron and Bing, who'd learned to tolerate each other's existence. If the review wound up being as awful as she anticipated, she'd need their comfort and commiseration.

"I hope her website isn't set to a different time zone," Janet offered with an all-knowing air. When the other Belles gawked at her in surprise, she added, "I'm taking an internet course at the community center. It's important to stay relevant."

Gail snorted. "You just want to learn how to use those fancy social media filters that erase all your wrinkles."

While the two women bickered, Abby gathered a calming breath, reminding herself that the review didn't matter. Whatever happened, she'd work it out—*they'd* work it out. She tightened her grip on Logan's hand, summoning a shaky smile. Together, they'd move forward and turn the inn into a success, with or without Serena's stamp of approval.

"There it is!" Nadia stabbed the screen, wrenching Abby's attention from her internal pep talk.

With another deep breath, she steeled herself for the worst and clicked on the article. Serena's blog post filled the screen, but Abby quickly averted her gaze.

"I can't do it." She snapped the laptop shut. "I can't read it. It's too much pressure. And in the big picture, it doesn't matter anyway, right?" So much for keeping her cool.

"True," Nadia agreed. "We all believe in you. We believe in this inn. But I think you'll regret not reading Serena's review."

Abby sighed. Nadia knew her too well. She needed to know what the article said. She flipped the laptop open. "You're right. But I still don't think I can read it. Will you do it?"

"Out loud?"

Abby nodded, digging her fingers into Logan's hand.

Nadia cleared her throat, and a collective hush settled around the room as she read Serena's words aloud.

"'When I first arrived at 1109 West State Street in Blessings Bay, California, I found smoke spilling out the window.'"

Abby winced, and Logan slung his arm around her shoulders.

Nadia flashed a reassuring smile that said *It'll be okay* and kept reading. "'Half a dozen women flitted across the front yard in a frenzy while a chubby English bulldog chased a lop-eared bunny around a tree.'"

"Chubby?" Verna huffed on Bing's behalf, completely missing the main concern—so far, Serena's review wasn't off to a great start.

"'Based on my first impression,'" Nadia continued, "'I had low expectations of Blessings on State Street and its innkeeper, Abigail Preston.'"

Abby's heart sank. She'd feared the worst and her fears had come to fruition. And yet, she'd foolishly held out hope for the impossible—that despite the initial hiccups, Serena had enjoyed her stay. That she'd felt welcomed. And whatever worries and burdens she'd brought with her had melted away. More than a perfect impression, she'd wanted to make a positive impact. And according to her own mission statement, she'd failed.

"'But that's the funny thing about expectations,'" Nadia read. "'More often than not, they're misguided. And in some cases, you're not only pleasantly surprised, you discover something special—something extraordinary—that you didn't even know you needed.'" Nadia paused, as if too stunned to speak, and Abby blinked, certain she'd misheard.

"Don't stop now!" Janet cried, fanning herself in excitement. "What else does it say?"

As Nadia continued, Abby's heart soared like she'd lift off the couch any second and float away.

"'Blessings on State Street isn't exceptional because the suites are luxurious and pristine or because the innkeeper's culinary prowess is unparalleled—although, you have to try her Monte Cristo Casserole at least once in your life. You can thank me later.'" Nadia paused as everyone chuckled, voicing their agreement, and Abby beamed.

"'This gem, situated on the stunning Northern California coastline, is my new favorite destination because checking in to Blessings on State Street feels like coming home. You're not simply a guest, you're part of the family. And in a world where strangers rarely smile and your neighbor doesn't know your name, personal connection is more important than ever. As someone who hasn't had a place to call home in a long time, I'd forgotten how much I yearned for a sense of belonging. Whether you need a quiet escape, romantic getaway, or a thrilling adventure, you'll find all you need and more in the magical town of Blessings Bay. Against the idyllic backdrop of spectacular sunsets and majestic waves is a community of people who genuinely care about each other, who will bring you into their fold in the best possible way. But be warned. Once you visit, you may never want to leave.'"

With the final word, Nadia lifted her gaze, her dark eyes glistening as if Serena's words resonated with her on a deeper level.

They spoke to Abby's heart, too.

"What do you think, Abs?" Nadia asked softly, turning the laptop screen to face her.

For the first time, Abby noticed the article's headline. "Blessings on State Street: The Unexpected Inn. How Checking In Will Change Your Life."

Abby smiled, tears blurring her vision as she glanced around the room, capturing a mental picture—a family portrait, imprinted on her heart.

But this portrait wasn't finished yet. How many more faces would be added in the days ahead?

She couldn't wait to find out.

Epilogue

SAGE HARPER CUPPED the smooth glass pebble in the palm of her hand, admiring the muted-blue sheen in the late afternoon sunlight. Not for the first time, she marveled at how a shard of shattered glass—tumbled and tossed in the waves for years on end—could become something so soft and beautiful. In her heartache, she clung to the metaphor, praying the tumultuous waves of life would subside, and she'd finally glimpse the beauty in her brokenness.

Laughter spilled down the beach, drawing her attention toward Abby, Logan, and Max. The blissful little family scoured the sand for shells and sea glass, competing to see who could collect the most. When Abby and Logan simultaneously spotted something in the sand, they each tried to reach it first, using any means necessary. Sage chuckled as Abby launched herself onto Logan's back, trying to weigh him down. Max wrapped himself around Logan's leg, but their collective efforts didn't seem to faze him.

As she watched the endearing scene unfold, happiness

warmed her heart. God had answered her prayers. Both for
Abby and Nadia.

She shifted her gaze offshore where Evan and Nadia
braved the frigid water in full-body wet suits. Sage grimaced
in sympathy as Nadia fell off her surfboard, plunging headfirst into the frothy surf. She must've wiped out a dozen
times already, but after each spill, Nadia climbed back on her
board and tried again. And for some unfathomable reason,
she seemed to be enjoying herself.

Sage tucked the small glass pebble in her back pocket.
Maybe she needed to take a page out of Nadia's playbook and
not give up so easily. Shielding her eyes from the sun, she
traced the crescent coastline toward the lighthouse shimmering at the tip of the cape. Its sleek silhouette reached
toward the sky, tall and reassuring—a beacon welcoming
seafarers home. A beacon of hope.

Hope.... A word laced with so many conflicting emotions.

Why did she find it so easy to have faith in other people's
dreams but couldn't believe in her own?

"Sage!" Abby jogged down the beach toward her, three
plastic buckets looped over her arm. "Will you tally our
bounty? Logan doesn't think I can be impartial." She tossed
a smirk over her shoulder, and Logan grinned back as he and
Max started building a sandcastle.

"Happy to help." Sage sat beside Abby while her friend
dumped the contents into three piles. The sun-kissed sand
felt warm against her bare feet, and she dug her toes deeper
into the silky granules, determined to savor the sweet, simple
moments.

"It's a perfect day, isn't it?" Abby murmured dreamily,
turning her face toward the sun. "I wish every spring could

be this warm, with the same bright, clear blue skies. Days like this are so cheerful."

"Do you think the cheeriness may also have something to do with recent events?" Sage teased, nudging her friend's shoulder with her own.

Abby's gaze drifted toward Max, and she smiled. "It might." Her features softened, and she glanced back at Sage. "What about you? You seem a little down about something."

Sage kneaded her bottom lip, not sure what to say. Today was about celebrating Max and the reunification of their family. She didn't want her personal problems to overshadow the joyful mood.

Sensing her hesitation, Abby prompted, "What happened, Sage? Is everything okay?"

Sage gathered a breath, grateful for Abby's caring heart. Maybe it would be better to confide in someone rather than keep the disappointment buried inside, festering. "I was so inspired by you and the inn, I decided to pursue one of my dreams, too."

"That's fantastic!" Abby beamed, sounding genuinely happy for her. "What is it?"

Sage hugged her knees to her chest, fanning her long peasant skirt around her ankles, stalling for time. She hadn't spoken her dream aloud since high school. Not since she'd shared it with her two dearest friends—her first love, Flynn, and his twin brother, Kevin. Her two greatest heartaches for very different reasons.

Steering her thoughts away from the murky waters of her past, she confessed, "I've always wanted to open a bookstore."

Abby clapped her hands together, her eyes glowing. "That's a lovely idea! I'm so excited for you."

"Thanks, but sadly, I don't think it's going to happen. I submitted my application for a business license, but it was rejected." The admission stung her throat, sharp, bitter, and difficult to swallow.

"What? Why?"

"The town council has a noncompete rule for new businesses. And since the Cahills already own a bookstore in town, they denied my application."

Never mind that she planned to sell completely different books. The Cahills' small selection couldn't be more niche. They sold only *New York Times* bestsellers, while she wanted to feature a wider range of lesser-known books—hidden gems in the literary world. But as one of the most prominent families in Blessings Bay, the Cahills had a knack for getting their way. And this wasn't the first time their interests had conflicted with her own.

Her thoughts drifted back to the dark corners of her memory—to Flynn Cahill. Even all these years later, the ache burned as intense as ever.

"I'm so sorry, Sage. There's nothing you can do?"

"Nothing that comes to mind." But she'd keep looking for a solution. She wasn't ready to give up just yet.

"Hey!" Logan hollered, oblivious to their serious conversation. "Can I pat myself on the back for winning yet?"

"Who says you won?" Abby challenged.

"I think Abby found the most," Max added his two cents, to which Logan playfully replied, "Hey, whose side are you on?"

Sage smiled at their lighthearted banter. She'd had that

once. With Flynn. But it felt like a lifetime ago. "Give me two seconds, and you can crown the winner." She counted each of the stacks, placing the shells and sea glass back into the buckets. "Uh-oh." She shot Abby a sympathetic grimace. "You and Logan are tied."

"Darn. I was really hoping to gloat. I had my winner's dance choreographed and everything."

Sage reached into her back pocket and pulled out the blue pebble. With a conspiratorial grin, she tossed it in the sand. "Oh, look. What's that?"

Abby grinned back and added the sea glass to her bucket.

"Whoa! Hang on! Cheater, cheater, pumpkin eater!" Logan called out in mock protest. "We saw that."

"Saw what?" Abby asked with feigned innocence.

"You know what happens to cheaters?" Logan asked Max.

Max shook his head, his brown eyes dancing with shared mischief.

"They're forced to walk the plank." Logan sprang to his feet, and Max gleefully followed. Abby shrieked with laughter, fleeing to save herself.

Sage observed their antics in amusement, wondering if Logan would actually toss Abby into the ice-cold water. She suspected he wouldn't. But without a doubt, they made the most adorable couple.

Logan caught Abby by the waist and hoisted her over his shoulder in a fireman's hold. Abby tried to protest but could barely squeak out a word between fits of laughter.

"Logan, don't you dare!" Nadia strode out of the water, surfboard in hand, cheeks flushed and glowing, coming to her friend's defense with a good-natured warning. Evan followed close behind, his blond hair slick with salt water. Sage had known him most of her life, and she could honestly say he'd never looked happier.

"Sorry, Nadia, but justice must be served." Logan stepped into the surf with his mirthful captive, but the loud blare of a foghorn halted their shenanigans.

A small fishing boat bobbed about a half mile offshore. A man shouted from the casting deck, but Sage couldn't quite make out the words. "What's he saying?"

"I think he said to call the coast guard," Evan said with a twinge of concern. "Sounds like they saw a shipwreck on one of the islands."

"Dad!" Max cheered. "They found my dad!"

Sage's heart lurched at his unflinching conviction.

Was it possible? Could the wreck really be Sam Bailey's boat?

And if so, what are the chances he survived?

CONTINUE THE STORY—and find out who owns the shipwrecked boat—in The Unbound Bookshop.

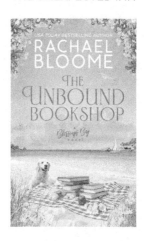

Abigail Preston's dreams are finally coming true... until a stranger appears on her doorstep with a secret from the past that turns her entire world upside down.

When **Sage Harper's** last chance to fulfill her childhood fantasy of owning a bookstore relies on living aboard a vintage sailboat for three days with her heartbreaker ex, she isn't sure she'll survive. Especially when she's reminded of all the reasons she fell in love with him in the first place....

Flynn Cahill, still haunted by the death of his twin brother, has dedicated his life to completing his brother's bucket list, even when it means losing the only woman he's ever loved.

When he finds himself stuck aboard a sailboat with the woman who still holds his heart, his plans for the future falter. Too bad, in her eyes, he's Enemy Number One.

Can they overcome past wounds and sail toward happily ever after? Or is any hope for romance lost at sea for good?

Acknowledgments

With each book I write, I'm continually amazed and thankful that I'm still here, doing what I love.

I owe special thanks and appreciation to my husband, Philip, and our family for helping me prioritize writing in between daily life and family adventures. And to my beautiful girls, V and V, for making motherhood so sweet. I'm so grateful to be your mom.

I'm also eternally grateful for Gwenn, Innkeeper Extraordinaire, for her inspiration and the phenomenal recipe behind Abby's Monte Cristo Casserole. It's her culinary prowess, not mine, that deserves all the credit.

Not only did Gwenn spark the original idea for this series, she continues to inspire me with her love, kindness, and strength. While I wrote this book, Gwenn was diagnosed with Stage 4 cancer—a diagnosis that could shake even the sturdiest foundation. But through it all, Gwenn has been a beacon of faith, hope, and light. She continues to care deeply for others, and it's this kind of strong, selfless love that I tried to infuse within the pages of this novel. So, if you ever read a book set in a town like Blessings Bay and think, "this sort of small town, where the people genuinely love and support one another, doesn't exist," please know that it does. And one such place is Jacksonville, Illinois, where you can stay in the very inn displayed on the cover of this book—Blessings on State Bed and Breakfast—where luxurious leisure meets hometown hospitality.

Book your stay today at blessingsonstate.com.

BLESSINGS ON STATE
BED & BREAKFAST

I'd also love to thank Ana Grigoriu-Voicu with Books-Design. Ana, you blew my mind with each Poppy Creek cover, and you've once again exceeded my expectations with Blessings Bay. Thank you for lending your creative brilliance to my beautiful book covers.

Heartfelt thanks to T London, my lovely beta reader, for her keen eye and encouraging words. To Krista Dapkey with KD Proofreading for sorting through my messy timeline and pesky compound words. And to Beth Attwood, for expertly combing through my manuscript for the countless errors that inevitably fall through the cracks. Without these wonderful ladies, my books would be comma-riddled cata-strophes. Or at least, not quite so polished.

Continued thanks to Dave Cenker, my incredible critique partner. Even though our lives get busy, and we can't always critique every word, I'm so grateful we're on this author journey together. And I can't wait to read your next book! Happy writing, my friend.

Much love and thanks to my dear ARC Team, who serves as the final and critical step to publication. You not only catch typos, you're pivotal in spreading the word about each new release. Your early reviews help assuage my fears and lend joy and excitement to an otherwise stressful time—aka Launch Day. I consider each of you as more than an advanced reader. You're a friend. And I'm beyond grateful you're part of my team.

And to my phenomenal readers, thank you! Whether we're visiting Poppy Creek or Blessings Bay or some other town I haven't yet created, I'm so thankful you're here with me, bringing the characters alive in your hearts.

May we have many more literary adventures ahead of us.

About the Author

Rachael Bloome is *USA Today* bestselling author and a *hopeful* romantic. She loves every moment leading up to the first kiss, as well as each second after saying, "I do." Torn between her small-town roots and her passion for traveling the world, she weaves both into her stories—and her life!

Joyfully living in her very own love story, she enjoys spending time with her loving husband, beautiful daughters, and two rescue dogs, Finley and Monkey. When she's not writing, helping to run the family coffee roasting business, or getting together with friends, she's busy planning their next big adventure!

Abby's Monte Cristo Casserole Recipe

A note from Innkeeper Gwenn:

Bed-and-breakfast innkeepers have many responsibilities and preparing breakfast is an important part of keeping our guests happy. (After all, it's part of our name!) This make-ahead breakfast bake is based on the traditional Monte Cristo sandwich, a French toast type sandwich brimming with meat and cheese.

Prep Time: 30 minutes

Bake Time: 1 hour

Serves: 8–10

Oven: 425° and 350°

INGREDIENTS

½ cup melted butter, divided

12 slices hearty white bread, crusts trimmed off

1 tbsp. mayonnaise mixed with 1 tsp. Dijon mustard

1 lb. premium smoked ham slices

1 lb. premium turkey breast slices

12 oz. shredded Gruyère and Swiss cheese (mixed)

½ tsp. ground black pepper

⅛ tsp. salt

5 eggs, beaten well

1 ½ cups half-and-half

4 oz. shredded Gruyère cheese, reserved

confectioner's sugar

½ cup red raspberry jam or red raspberry syrup

THE NIGHT BEFORE:

Step 1:

Gather your ingredients. Start with two 13x9″ pans, one of which should stack just inside the top of the other. If you don't have two deep pans that will work together, you may use a small rimmed baking sheet, i.e., a jelly roll pan, instead. Place the smaller pan on a rack in the middle of the oven and preheat to 425°F as your build the sandwiches.

Step 2:

Prepare sandwiches. Pour ¼ cup melted butter in the bottom of the second (larger) pan. Spread the mayonnaise and Dijon mustard mixture on one side of six slices of bread. Arrange the bread, mayo side up, in the baking pan.

Step 3:

Cover the bread with turkey and ham, alternating layers, then sprinkle heavily with the cheese mixture. Season with salt and pepper.

Step 4:

Top each "sandwich" with remaining bread slices, then brush tops with reserved melted butter.

Step 5:

Using oven mitts, very carefully remove the preheated baking pan from the oven and place, rimmed side up, on top of sandwiches. Holding both baking pans together with sandwiches in between, return to the oven. Bake until the bread is browned and cheese melted, about 15 minutes.

Step 6:

Remove from the oven and let cool. In the meantime, beat the eggs and whisk in the half-and-half. Pour over the cooled sandwiches, coating the tops of each sandwich as you pour. (The very top of the top crusts should be coated as you pour, but should not end up fully covered by the egg mixture in the pan.) Cover with foil and refrigerate overnight.

90 MINUTES BEFORE SERVING:

Preheat oven to 350°. Uncover and sprinkle the top with the remaining Gruyère cheese. Re-cover with foil and bake the casserole at 350° for 50 minutes.

Uncover and bake for 15 minutes or until sandwiches are browned and the egg mixture is set.

Sprinkle with confectioner's sugar and serve with raspberry jam or raspberry syrup for a tasty sweet and savory breakfast.

Enjoy!

Book Club Questions

1. Which character did you identify with the most? And why?

2. Why do you think Abby feels so much pressure to make the inn successful? Was there a time in your life when you felt a similar pressure, whether external or internal?

3. Logan struggles to feel worthy and whole in light of his injury. Can you relate to those emotions? Have you ever struggled to accept help from others?

4. Nadia believes finding her perfect match will solve her relationship problems. What lesson do you think she learned? And do you agree or disagree?

5. Both Evan and Nadia share a personal connection to a treat their mother made. For Nadia, it's chai. For Evan, taffy. Is there a food or beverage that holds special meaning to you?

6. At first, Evan interpreted Nadia's review as harsh criticism. Over time, he saw the truth and kindness in her words. Was there a moment in your life where someone told you a hard truth, but you later realized they said it from a place of love?

7. What did you think of Serena's character? Do you think Abby handled the situation well? How would you have reacted in her shoes?

8. Evan lost sight of his own passions and purpose when he took over his mother's business, focusing solely on continuing her legacy. Have you ever let someone else's expectations or influence determine your life choices? Did it turn out to be a help or hindrance?

9. Bonnie tells Evan that Blessings Bay feels like home because the people have become her family and they "care about each other in sincere, actionable ways. They live out their love, even when it costs them something." What do you think makes a place feel like home?

10. Evan tells Nadia "No man—not Brian, not me, not anyone—can define your worth." Do you think his statement is true? Why or why not?

11. When Abby is faced with losing Max, she has this reaction: *She wanted to shout,* But we *are* his family. *But what good would that do? She knew what Carla meant. They weren't blood. And when it came to the blood, sweat, and tears of raising a child, blood always won*. Do you think this statement is true? What do you think makes a family?

12. What do you think Nadia's mother meant by the following statement: "I want more for you than a comfortable life. More than happiness, even. I want you to have a *full* life, filled with all the greatness God has for you."

13. Nadia says Evan is the bravest man she knows because "when it comes to matters of the heart, he doesn't hold back." What do you think makes someone brave?

14. What do you think is the main theme of the novel? Why?

As always, I look forward to hearing your thoughts on the story. You can email your responses (or ask your own questions) at hello@rachaelbloome.com or post them in my private Facebook group, Rachael Bloome's Secret Garden Book Club.

Also by Rachael Bloome

Rachael Bloome
STORIES WITH HEART & HOPE

POPPY CREEK SERIES

The Clause in Christmas

The Truth in Tiramisu

The Secret in Sandcastles

The Meaning in Mistletoe

The Faith in Flowers

The Whisper in Wind

The Hope in Hot Chocolate

The Promise in Poppies

STANDALONE NOVELS

New York, New Year, New You

Made in the USA
Las Vegas, NV
06 May 2024

89606362R00166